BO JACKSON

BY JOHN ROLFE

A *SPORTS ILLUSTRATED FOR KIDS* BOOK

Written by John Rolfe
Cover photograph by Allsport USA / Mike Powell
Cover design by Pegi Goodman
Interior line art by Jane Davila
Produced by Angel Entertainment, Inc.

SPORTS ILLUSTRATED FOR KIDS is a trademark of THE TIME INC.
MAGAZINE COMPANY

SPORTS ILLUSTRATED FOR KIDS Books is a joint imprint of Little, Brown and Company and Warner Juvenile Books.

Printed in the United States of America

First Printing: May 1991
10 9 8 7 6 5 4 3 2 1

Published simultaneously in Canada by Little, Brown & Company (Canada) Limited

Library of Congress Cataloging-in-Publication Data

Rolfe, John
   Bo Jackson / John Rolfe.
      p.   cm.
   "A sports illustrated for kids book."
   Summary: A biography of the star athlete who plays both professional baseball and football.
    ISBN 0-316-75457-9 (pbk.)
    1. Jackson, Bo, 1962-   —Juvenile literature. 2. Baseball players — United States — Biography — Juvenile Literature.
   [1. Jackson, Bo, 1962-   . 2. Baseball players. 3. Football players. 4. Afro-Americans — Biography.] I. Title.
   GV865.J28R65 1991
   [92]—dc20   90-55742
                                                   CIP
                                                   AC

Contents

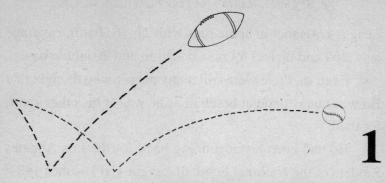

1

The Star of All Stars

When outfielder Bo Jackson of the Kansas City Royals went to bat in the first inning of the 1989 baseball All-Star Game, the crowd of 64,036 fans cheered loudly. Millions of people around the country leaned closer to their TV sets. There were many great players on the field in Anaheim Stadium on July 11, 1989, but Bo was the one whom people particularly wanted to see.

Bo's at-bat was special. He was playing in his first major league All-Star Game and he had received more All-Star votes from fans than any other American League player.

Bo deserved to be an All-Star. He was the American

1

League co-leader in home runs with 21. His batting average was .265 and he had 59 runs batted in and 20 stolen bases.

Even so, there were still many people who thought that Bo was not as good at baseball as he was at his other sport: football.

Bo had been a star running back for the Los Angeles Raiders of the National Football League (NFL) since 1987. He had also been a college All-America running back who won the Heisman Trophy in 1985. The Heisman is given each year to the best college football player in the country.

Even though Bo had also been an excellent baseball player in high school and college, he had not been as successful in professional baseball as people had thought he would be. Bo had struggled during his first two seasons with the Royals. He often struck out and he made a lot of fielding errors.

Fans and sportswriters said that Bo would never be a great major league player until he quit football and concentrated only on baseball. Those people who thought that Bo could not succeed in both sports did not understand one very important thing about him: when Bo Jackson is told that he cannot do something, he becomes very determined to prove that he can — and he usually does.

"Ever since I was little, people doubted what I was going to accomplish," Bo says. "My childhood made me a very determined man."

So when Bo went to bat for the first time in the 1989 All-Star Game, he was very determined to prove that he could be a great major league player.

Bo stepped into the batter's box, cocked his bat with his muscular arms, and waited for the first pitch from Rick Reuschel of the National League All-Star Team.

Reuschel's first pitch was a strike. Bo took a deep breath and got ready again. Reuschel's next pitch was low and on the inside part of the plate. Bo reached down as he swung and hit a towering fly ball to centerfield. Eric Davis, the National League centerfielder, took one step back and then stopped.

Bo's fly ball kept going, and going, and going. When it landed deep in the stands, nearly 450 feet from home plate, the crowd went wild! Former President Ronald Reagan, who was known as "The Great Communicator" because he was a very talented speaker, was a guest TV announcer at the game. All he could say about Bo's home run was, "Oh! Oh!"

Bo's home run made him only the ninth player to ever hit a home run in his first at-bat in an All-Star Game. There was more to come. Bo's great night had just begun.

In the second inning, Bo came up to bat again. There was one out, the American League had runners on first base and third base, and the score was tied 2-2. Bo hit a grounder to shortstop Ozzie Smith, who grabbed it and tried to make a double play. Smith threw to second baseman Ryne Sandberg to get one out, but Bo beat Sandberg's throw to first base, and the runner on third scored. The American League was ahead 3-2.

Bo then tried to steal second base. He knew it wouldn't be easy because National League catcher Benito Santiago had a strong throwing arm. When Bo took off, Santiago panicked and threw the ball into centerfield. Bo then became the first player since Hall of Famer Willie Mays in 1960 to hit a home run *and* steal a base in one All-Star Game!

During the game, a new TV commercial was shown. It starred Bo and a group of famous athletes who all said something about Bo's abilities. Runner Joan Benoit Samuelson said, "Bo knows running." Chicago Bulls basketball star Michael Jordan said, "Bo knows basketball." Jim Everett of the Los Angeles Rams said, "Bo knows football." Kirk Gibson of the Los Angeles Dodgers said, "Bo knows baseball."

Bo was the first player to bat after the commercial, and he proved again that he really did know baseball. Bo hit a line drive for a single. It was his second hit of the game. The American League went on to win, 5-3, and Bo was named the game's Most Valuable Player!

Many fans, sportswriters, and even the National League All-Stars were amazed by what Bo had done. "I don't think I've seen anybody combine power and speed like that since Mickey Mantle," said National League manager Tom Lasorda of the Los Angeles Dodgers. "He has a chance to be one of the greatest ever to play this game. He's awesome."

National League outfielder Tony Gwynn, who plays for the San Diego Padres, said, "For me, one of the best reasons for coming here was to see what Bo could do. Bo can do anything. He's scary."

Sportswriter Tom McEwen wrote in the *Tampa* (Florida) *Tribune*, "Many people who thought Bo couldn't play baseball and football at the same time are having second thoughts now. I'm one of them. I admire him."

Bo wasn't amazed by what he had done. "People don't know what I can do," he said. "I know what Bo can do. I know he can play football and baseball."

Indeed he can. That's why Bo Jackson is now one of the most famous athletes in the world. Bo can do amazing things in every sport he plays.

Bo Can Do Amazing Things in Football:

• Bo is the first running back in NFL history to run more than 90 yards for a touchdown two times.

• Bo has gained an average of 5.3 yards each time he has run with the ball for the Raiders. That average is the highest in the history of the NFL!

Bo Can Do Amazing Things in Baseball:

• In 1988, Bo became the first player in Royals history to hit 25 home runs and steal 25 bases in one season.

• Bo hit 79 home runs during his first three full major league seasons. Hank Aaron, who is the all-time major league home run champion, hit 66 during his first three seasons!

Bo Can Do Amazing Things in Track and Field:

• Bo set Alabama state high school records in the 60-yard and 120-yard hurdles, the long jump, and the high jump.

• Bo won Alabama state high school championships in the triple jump and the decathlon, in which athletes compete in the 100-meter sprint, long jump, shot put, high jump, 400-meter run, 110-meter hurdles, discus, pole vault, javelin, and 1500-meter run.

Many athletes have played more than one amateur or professional sport, but Bo is one of the very few who have become *stars* in more than one. The most famous examples are Jim Thorpe and Mildred "Babe" Didrikson Zaharias.

Thorpe won two gold medals in track and field at the 1912 Olympics and he played in the NFL from 1915 to 1929. Thorpe was later elected to the Pro Football Hall of Fame. He also played in the major leagues from 1913 to 1919, but he was not as successful in baseball.

Babe Didrikson Zaharias won two gold medals and one silver medal in track at the 1932 Olympics. She was also an All-America basketball player and the winner of three U. S. Open Golf Championships.

Bo Jackson is the first athlete who has ever starred in both pro baseball and pro football at the same time! Each year, Bo plays for the Royals from March to October. Then he plays for the Raiders from October to the end of the season in either December or January. Before Bo began doing that in 1987, no one since 1954 had even *tried* to play those two pro sports at the same time.

Perhaps the most amazing thing of all about Bo is that he rarely works out or trains hard! Bo owns $13,000 worth of weight equipment that he rarely uses, but his body is packed with solid muscle. Bo is 6'1", he weighs 222 pounds, and he can bench press 400 pounds.

After the baseball season each year, Bo spends 10 days preparing to play football by taking long walks with his wife, Linda. Other NFL players prepare by working out in training camp for seven grueling weeks each summer!

In 1987, Bo was drafted by the Orange County (California) Crush of the International Basketball Association even though he had never played organized basketball. Why? Because Bo can jump three feet straight up in the air. Only basketball players like Michael Jordan jump that high!

As talented as he is, Bo did have to learn that even the most gifted athletes must practice. For many years, Bo succeeded in sports solely on his natural ability. He later realized that he could not make the most of his ability if he did not practice. After that, Bo became a superstar.

8

Bo now earns millions of dollars playing for the Royals and the Raiders. He is also paid millions of dollars to advertise several products. Bo drives an expensive Ferrari Testarossa™ sports car and he owns two big houses. One of them is in his hometown of Bessemer, Alabama. The other is in Leawood, Kansas.

Bo is now so famous that a street in Bessemer has been named Bo Jackson Avenue. There is a 60-foot-high picture of him on the side of a building in Hollywood, California. "Bo knows" is a popular expression. He is mobbed by fans wherever he goes.

Bo's fame and talent make it hard to think of him as a "regular guy." People expect Bo to do spectacular things whenever he plays. They expect him to sign autographs and do interviews every time he is asked. Many people do not realize that Bo is actually just a quiet man who wants to live a normal life with his wife and children when he is not playing sports.

"I would rather not have people know about my personal life," he says. "Once I leave the stadium, I don't belong to the public anymore."

Bo is so serious about guarding his privacy that he does

not even give his home phone number to the teams he plays for. If they have to reach him to change a practice time, they call his agent. He receives so much attention from reporters and fans that he often feels uncomfortable. And it's not only because of the *amount* of attention he receives. It is because Bo used to stutter whenever he spoke.

"When I was little, I used to stutter so bad I wouldn't talk in public because people would laugh," Bo says. "I was a real bad stutterer until my freshman year in college."

Bo has learned to control his stutter, but he still does not feel at ease when he talks to reporters and people he does not know. "The hardest part of my job is dealing with the press," he says. "People say I'm arrogant just because I didn't talk to them. I'm just not a very talkative person."

When Bo does talk to reporters, he often sounds conceited because he refers to himself as "Bo" and not "me" or "I." Bo does that because it is easier for him to say "Bo" without stuttering than to say "I."

People also misunderstand Bo because he is very confident. In 1987, when he said that pro football was his hobby, he was booed by fans and criticized by his teammates and by sportswriters who thought he was saying that he could play in the NFL without even trying.

"What I meant is that I plan to make a career out of baseball," Bo says. "I know football is a serious job."

Bo believes that he can succeed at anything he wants to do. "Playing two sports has nothing to do with trying to be the world's greatest athlete," he says. "I don't think you should put limits on what a person can accomplish."

Bo loves sports and he has a lot of fun playing them. Yet people have accused him of playing two pro sports only because he is greedy. "I know people have got the wrong impression," Bo says. "I'm not doing this to get all the money I can. This is just the way I want to spend my time."

Joe Scannella, who is one of Bo's coaches on the Raiders, says, "Do you want to know what Bo really is? He's just a regular guy who is playing two sports."

Bo likes to go hunting and fishing. He enjoys going to theaters to see plays. Most of all, Bo loves being at home with Linda, who is a child psychologist, and their children, Garrett, who was born in 1986, Nicholas, who was born in 1988, and Morgan, who was born in 1990. "When I leave the ballpark, I become a husband and a father," Bo says. "That's a side of me the public never sees."

When Bo travels with the Royals or the Raiders, he calls home as many as four times a day just to talk with Linda and their kids. Bo is often exhausted when he gets home after his games, but he is never too tired to play with Morgan, Nicholas, and Garrett.

When Nicholas was born, Bo cried with joy the first time he held his new son. "I could see the look on the nurse's face," Linda says. "She was shocked that this was Bo Jackson and that he was so human and so nice."

People can be shocked to learn that Bo is nice because he rarely talks about the kind and generous things he does. For example, Bo did not tell anyone about the time when he was in college that he stopped at the scene of an accident and pulled an injured woman out of a car that was smoking and possibly about to explode.

"Bo is that kind of person," says Royals outfielder Willie Wilson. "He doesn't like to be the center of attention, but when it comes to helping people, he's softhearted. People don't realize what a good person he is, but he's one of the finest persons I've ever known."

Royals pitcher Tom Gordon agrees. When Gordon joined the Royals in 1989, he was a nervous rookie who did not have a place to live in Kansas City. Bo invited Gordon to stay at his home until he found a house of his own.

"Bo made me feel like I was somebody," Gordon says. "He helped me out like I was his own kid."

Bo *loves* kids. He works for a charity that helps kids who have trouble reading and learning in school. "Bo is special," says Don Fitzpatrick, the manager of the visiting team clubhouse in Boston's Fenway Park. "He's one of the few players I've ever seen who tips each clubhouse kid. [He was referring to the young people who tend to the clubhouse and make sure that the players' equipment is organized.] Not only that, he talks to each of them about staying in school and staying away from drugs."

"I'm determined to get as many kids as I can to turn their heads away from drugs," Bo says. "People who take drugs are crazy. I hate to see so many guys in the major leagues waste their time and money that way. What they do affects a lot of kids."

Famous athletes do not always want to be role models for kids. Bo feels that being a good role model is very important. "Kids need someone to teach them right from wrong," he says. "When I was growing up, no one took the time to talk to me or tell me what was right. I know kids will listen to me, that's why I make time for them."

Playing sports, and being a great athlete and a real person are what Bo is all about. "Some people say that just because I'm Bo Jackson, I'm not supposed to be human," he says. "Once they get to know me, they say 'Wow!' because they didn't think I hung around with normal people."

No matter what people say or think about him, Bo is determined to be himself. "People are always going to criticize me," he says, "but I don't hear the boos. I don't hear the cheers. I never read the sports pages. I live my life for Bo, just like you live your life for you. I'm not going to try to change what people think of me. I'm just going to be Bo."

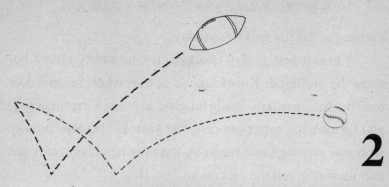

2

The Neighborhood Bully

Bo has not always been Bo. His mother named him Vincent Edward Jackson when he was born on November 30, 1962, in Bessemer, Alabama. Vincent was the eighth of 10 children. He lived in Raimund, a small country town near Bessemer, until he was 8 years old.

Vincent lived in a small, three-room house with his four brothers, five sisters, and his mother, Florence. His father, A.D. Adams, had never married Florence and he did not live with the family.

Mrs. Jackson worked long hours as a maid at a local motel, but she still had trouble earning enough money to buy food for her 10 children. There were times when they had nothing to eat for almost two days.

Vincent was a very quiet child who rarely talked because he stuttered. Kids laughed at him when he spoke or read out loud in class. Being laughed at made Vincent angry, and he took his anger out on other kids. He became a bully who was so tough and mean by the time he was 6 years old that he was given the nickname "Bo Hog."

"Bo Hog" was short for "Boar Hog." (A boar hog is a wild pig that is often vicious.) Vincent's brothers and cousins thought of the nickname after they were unable to hurt him by punching him in the stomach as hard as they could. "Bo Hog" later became "Bo," the name Vincent Jackson is known by today.

Bo lived up to his nickname in grade school. He stole money from his mother and his classmates. He paid kids to beat up others. He even hit one of his cousins with a baseball bat after she took a ping pong paddle away from him!

"By third grade, I was so bad I'd bully the sixth graders," Bo says. "Breaking windows, beating up kids, stealing bikes, throwing rocks, that's what I was known for. You name it, I did it."

Bo got into trouble a lot and his mother was often very

angry at him. She punished him by making him wake up before dawn to mow the lawn or take out the garbage.

Bo spent a lot of time mowing the lawn and taking out the garbage, but he kept getting into trouble no matter how often he was punished. His mom did everything she could to make Bo change, but it was difficult for her to watch him because she had to work. That made it easy for Bo to roam the streets and make the wrong kind of friends.

"My father lived across town and I had three older brothers and they always seemed to be away, too," Bo says. "I had no one to really talk to. I fought with my sisters, so I ran loose with a tough bunch of kids."

As you might expect, Bo was tempted to do drugs. He tried smoking marijuana, but it made him so hungry that he ate everything in his refrigerator. Then he fell asleep. When he woke up, he got sick to his stomach. Bo says that he never did drugs again, but he found plenty of other bad things to do.

Bo did not stop until he got into so much trouble that his mom threatened to send him to reform school. Bo was 13 years old when his life changed on a summer day in 1976.

Bo and his friends were walking to a pond to go

swimming when they passed the home of a minister who had a hog pen in his yard. Bo and his friends started throwing rocks and bricks at the hogs. They hit the hogs with sticks and killed several of them.

When a man who watched the house for the minister saw what Bo and his friends were doing, he fired a gun at them! Bo and his friends ran away, but the man recognized Bo. He told the minister what Bo had done. When the minister told Mrs. Jackson, she was furious. She told the minister, "If you want to send Bo to reform school, go ahead. I can't do a thing with him."

The minister decided that it would be better if Bo worked to earn enough money to repay him for the hogs that had been killed. Mrs. Jackson agreed, and Bo was grounded for the rest of the summer, which meant that he had to work or be at home and that he couldn't roam the streets. He spent his time doing chores and listening to his mother tell him that he would one day end up in prison if he did not change. Bo got the message.

"My mom had a lot of influence on me, because she refused to let us kids dodge responsibility for what we did," Bo says. "She said I wouldn't amount to anything unless I straightened out. Once I made that decision, I found I could do almost anything I set my mind on."

The first thing Bo set his mind on was sports. He had been a good athlete since first grade, which was when he began playing baseball in neighborhood games. When Bo was in third grade, he ran sprints with a team of older kids one day. When Bo outran them, the team's coach let him stay with the team even though only fourth, fifth, and sixth graders were allowed to be on it.

When Bo was making trouble, he forgot all about sports. So when he finally decided to settle down, he rediscovered his athletic talent. He spent a lot of time at the local playground and he learned how competitive he was.

"I always wanted to be better than anyone else," Bo says. "If someone jumped over a fence, I did it too, or stayed there until I did. That was my attitude in everything."

When Bo entered ninth grade at McAdory High School, he asked his mother if he could try out for the football team. Mrs. Jackson said no at first because she was afraid that Bo would get hurt. She finally agreed, but she refused to go to Bo's games.

Bo made the football team easily. He later tried out for

track and baseball and made those teams easily, too. Bo spent so much time playing sports that year that he was too tired to hang around with his old group of friends. "I made new friends that didn't get into trouble," he says.

Bo's coaches saw how dedicated he was to sports. "He went to school, he practiced whatever sport was in season, and he went home," says Dick Atchison, who was the football coach at McAdory High. "That was it."

Bo did not *always* practice the sports he played, but he had so much natural talent that he was good at them anyway. Bo could throw a three-pound, nine-ounce discus 150 feet — a competitive distance for a high school athlete — even though he had never been taught the proper way to throw it. He was a good hurdler and long jumper, despite the fact that McAdory High did not have track facilities where Bo could learn and practice those skills. Bo had to practice hurdling by jumping over folding chairs!

"Bo can watch somebody do something and then do it himself," says Coach Atchison. "You have to pole vault in the decathlon. Bo never touched a pole until the day he walked out on the track. After about three tries, he looked like he had been pole vaulting all his life."

Bo's coaches were amazed by how good he was in sports in which he did not even compete. Bo could do flips off a diving board, and he was a good swimmer. He could pick up a tennis racket and defeat players who were on the school's varsity tennis team. He could dunk a basketball.

Terry Brasseale, who was McAdory High's baseball coach, saw Bo sitting alone in the school gym one day. Bo noticed a basketball that was lying on the floor and he walked over and picked up the ball. Bo made sure no one was around before he took a couple of steps and dunked the ball behind his head. Then he picked up his books and went home.

"I guess he just wanted to see if he could do it," Coach Brasseale says.

Bo improved steadily in every sport he played, especially track. He finished 10th in the Alabama State Decathlon Championship as a freshman. As a sophomore, he finished second. Then he won the state decathlon championship as a junior and a senior.

Bo did so many things so well that at various times he played outfield, shortstop, and pitcher on the McAdory baseball team. In football, Bo could play running back, defensive end, kicker, and kick returner.

During Bo's junior year, people learned about all the things he did. Newspaper stories were written about him and colleges sent scouts to watch him play. But Bo's three older brothers tried to make him stop playing so many sports.

"They said I couldn't succeed in three sports and that I should stick with one and stop trying to impress my friends and the people in the community," Bo says. "I told them it was none of their business what I did."

Bo's brothers only made him more determined to succeed. His determination helped him do spectacular things during his senior year at McAdory High. Bo led the football team to a record of nine wins and no losses, and he won All-State honors as a running back. Bo gained 1,173 yards, even though he carried the ball only 108 times that season. That means Bo gained an average of almost 11 yards each time he carried the ball! Major colleges in Alabama, Florida, California, Nebraska, and Hawaii offered him football scholarships.

Bo got a lot of attention during his senior year, but he found it difficult to talk to the scouts and reporters who were so interested in him, and the students who admired him. He often sat by himself in a corner of the gym and studied while other kids sat and talked somewhere else. Bo wasn't being a snob — he was shy. By then, he had become more likeable than ever before.

"Midway through 12th grade, Bo changed," says Coach Brasseale. "He started being real nice to everybody. As a sophomore and a junior, he had a chip on his shoulder."

Bo's schoolmates saw how much he had changed after McAdory High's outstanding athlete was announced at a pep rally after the football season. When a white athlete won the award instead of Bo, some of the black players on the football team became very angry. They refused to stand and applaud the winner. That made some of the white football players angry.

It seemed that a fight was going to break out, so the school's principal ordered all the seniors to meet in the library. When the meeting began, everyone in the library was tense and angry. Then Bo asked to speak. The room grew quiet. "I didn't come to school here to get all the glory and win trophies," Bo said. "I came here for education. You all better get your acts together."

When Bo finished speaking, the other kids made up

with each other. "Everyone was hugging," says Coach Bras-seale. "It was quite a thing. That's Bo Jackson."

During the spring semester that year, Bo set a school high jump record of 6'9". He also won the state decathlon championship. In baseball, Bo pitched two no-hitters. His batting average was .447 and he set a national high school record by hitting 20 home runs, even though he missed seven games because he had competed in track meets instead.

Each day, Bo played the sport that gave him the greatest challenge. For example, one day a group of major league scouts went to see Bo play baseball. Bo knew the scouts were coming to see him and that he would be drafted by a big league team if he played well that day. Bo competed in a track meet that day instead. Why? Because there was a very good runner on the other school's team whom Bo wanted to beat, and he did!

Bo had a big decision to make that spring. Did he want to attend college on a football or track scholarship, or did he want to play pro baseball instead?

At first, Bo was tempted to choose pro baseball when the New York Yankees offered him $220,000 to play for one of their minor league teams. They also invited Bo and his mother to New York so he could take batting practice at Yankee Stadium and sit in the Yankee dugout during a game. Bo's mother refused the offer.

"I'm not going to New York," she said. "I don't need their money. I raised ten kids without their money. Their money doesn't mean anything to me."

A lot of people told Bo that he was crazy to listen to his mom. Bo chose to attend college anyway. "My mother told me I can have money for a short time, but education is for my whole life," Bo says. "My mother was proud when I signed a full scholarship at Auburn. I was the first from my family to attend a major college."

Bo chose Auburn University by accident. At first, he planned to attend the University of Alabama.

Alabama was famous for its great football teams that were coached by Paul "Bear" Bryant, who was one of the most successful coaches in college football history. Bryant won 323 games and lost only 85 during his career, and his Alabama Crimson Tide teams won six national championships. Bo rooted for Alabama while he was growing up and he had dreamed about playing for "The Tide."

Bo changed his mind after Ken Donohue, who was one

of Coach Bryant's assistants, said that Bo would not play for The Tide until his junior year because there were too many good players on the team. Bo wanted to play college football right away, so he decided to go to Auburn instead.

Auburn was one of Alabama's biggest rivals, but its football teams had not been as successful. Auburn had won only one national championship in 90 years. It had not even won a Southeastern Conference (SEC) Championship since 1957, and it had not beaten Alabama in football since 1972.

Even so, Bo liked Auburn University the first time he visited it. The school's campus was in Auburn, Alabama, and it was only 85 miles away from Bessemer. Best of all, Auburn's football coach said that Bo could play football right away and also run track and play baseball.

When Bo told Ken Donahue that he was going to attend Auburn, Donohue said, "Bo, if you go to Auburn, you'll never beat Alabama."

As you might guess, Ken Donahue later wished that he had never said that to Bo Jackson.

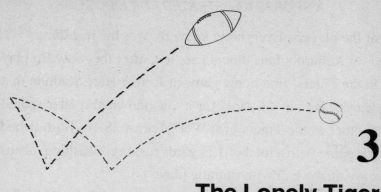

3

The Lonely Tiger

Bo arrived at Auburn University for football practice in the summer of 1982. Even though he had been a football star in high school, his coaches thought that he would be just another freshman running back. It didn't take long for Bo to show them that they were wrong.

Bo's first scrimmage, or practice game, was against the Auburn Tigers' starting defense. Bo gained an average of 12 yards each time he ran with the ball! He shook off tacklers and ran over defenders who were bigger than he was.

"Bo ran wild," says Bobby Wallace, who was one of Auburn's secondary coaches. "There was electricity in the air. The coaches could feel it. You could see it in the eyes of the players. Everybody knew Bo was the real thing."

Auburn's fans thought so, too, after they saw Bo play in the Tigers' first home game at Jordan-Hare Stadium that season. Bo ran 43 yards for a touchdown and later scored another as the Tigers beat Wake Forest 28-10. Bo finished the game with a total of 123 yards rushing. (Rushing means moving the ball with running plays.)

Sportswriters and fans then compared Bo to Herschel Walker. Walker was an All-America running back for the University of Georgia. In 1980, Walker set a college record for freshmen by gaining 1,616 yards. In 1981, he set a college record for sophomores by gaining 1,891 yards. Today, Walker plays in the NFL for the Minnesota Vikings.

Bo didn't like being compared to the best player in college football. "Nobody can be Herschel Walker but Herschel, and I can't be anybody but myself," Bo said.

That was true, but Bo had made it easier for people to compare him to Walker when he asked to wear number 34 on his football jersey. Walker also wore number 34. Bo even ran like Walker and gained 100 yards or more in three of his first five games. The Tigers won four of them, and Bo became a star.

Bo did not feel like a star in the classroom or on campus that fall. He still stuttered, so he kept to himself even though he shared a mobile home near Auburn with his teammate, running back Lionel James. James was a friendly guy who loved parties. Bo liked James, but he felt awkward at parties. Bo usually stayed in his room and listened to gospel music instead.

That fall, Bo spent so much time alone that he began to realize how unhappy he was. Bo was having trouble getting good grades and he was homesick because he had never been away from home before. He also hated football practice.

Bo had not practiced football very hard in high school, so he was shocked by how tough the Tiger practices were each day. The team's coaches often pushed players as hard as they could in practice; they yelled at Bo whenever he made mistakes or was lazy.

Being yelled at made Bo so unhappy that he decided to leave Auburn one afternoon in November of 1982. Bo packed his bags and borrowed a friend's car. He then drove to a local bus station. He was about to take a bus back home when something made him stop.

"I started thinking of all the people back home and what

they expected of me," Bo says. "They expected great things. I realized that I had been given an opportunity, and that I would let people down if I ran away from it."

Bo sat in the bus station for six hours before he was told to leave. Bo then drove back to Auburn. When his coaches learned what he had done, they made him run up and down the grandstand steps in Jordan-Hare Stadium 100 times! Pat Dye, the Tigers' head coach, later told him, "Bo, your presence on this football team gives Auburn people hope."

Bo felt better after that, and he decided to stay with the team. He knew he had made the right decision after the Tigers played Alabama in the final game of the regular season that year.

The game was a big one. The Crimson Tide players wanted to win because Bear Bryant was going to retire as their head coach after the season. The Tigers wanted to win because they had not beaten The Tide in 10 years. Bo *really* wanted to win because Ken Donahue had said that Auburn would never beat Alabama.

There were only two minutes and thirty seconds left in the game when Bo made Donahue eat his words. The Tigers were losing, 22-17, but they had the ball on Alabama's one-yard line. It was fourth down, and the Tigers needed a touchdown to win the game. If their play failed, it was very likely that they would lose.

Bo then took a handoff and he leaped toward the goal line. He was met by a wall of Crimson Tide defenders, but he kept struggling forward until he crossed the goal line for a touchdown! Auburn hung on to win 23-22.

"Whatever that coach said got Bo to go just one more inch, and that one inch made all the difference," said David Housel, who was Auburn's sports information director.

The Tigers' record that season was nine wins and only three losses. Bo gained 829 yards rushing and he won All-Southeastern Conference Honors.

Bo joined Auburn's track and baseball teams the following spring. He became the first SEC athlete since 1967 to letter in more than two sports.

In track, Bo was a member of Auburn's 4 x 100-meter relay team. He also ran the 60-yard dash. Bo's best time in that event (6.18 seconds) qualified him to compete in the National Collegiate Indoor Championships that spring. Bo was a semi-finalist in the 60-yard dash at that meet.

Bo enjoyed his freshman season in track. He could

relax and have fun because his track coaches did not yell at him all the time. Bo enjoyed track so much that year he told reporters that it was his favorite sport.

"I like track because you can't blame your defeats on ten other guys," Bo said. "You have to kick yourself in the butt and go on. If I could turn pro in track, I would."

People were surprised when Bo said that because they thought of him as a football star who would automatically play in the NFL after college. But Bo was a better track athlete than most people realized.

"If Bo had decided to concentrate solely on track, he could have been an Olympic sprinter," said Mel Rosen, Auburn's track coach.

Bo did not enjoy baseball that spring as much as he had hoped. He did not get along very well with the team's coach, and he also struck out the first 21 times he went to bat. "I wondered if I would ever hit the ball again in my lifetime," Bo says.

Bo finally hit the ball the 22nd time he went to bat and it sailed over the fence for a home run! Bo batted .279 and he hit four home runs that season.

Bo's life at Auburn was more enjoyable during his

sophomore year, especially after his football coaches started to ease up on him in practice.

The Tiger coaches had been unhappy because Bo did not practice hard even though he had many skills to polish. They also did not like Bo's habit of falling asleep in the locker room before games while the other players were getting pumped up to play. When Bo played well anyway, the coaches realized that they did not need to push him as hard as they pushed the other players.

Coach Dye said, "I'm not going to question Bo as long as he is not a distraction to the other coaches and players." The coaches were worried that the other players would resent Bo if he did not have to practice as long and as hard as they did. They stopped worrying when they saw that Bo's teammates liked and trusted him.

"Everybody knows Bo will be there on Saturdays when it counts," said Tiger running back Tommie Agee.

"I don't know of any resentment," said Bud Casey, who was one of the Tigers' assistant coaches. "The players know Bo is a good guy who doesn't smoke, doesn't drink, doesn't do drugs, and strives to get good grades."

Coach Dye said, "I think all the coaches and players

accepted Bo for the way he is and the kind of guy he is."

Bo was much happier after that, and he played harder than ever. Bo gained 196 yards against Florida, even though he was sick with a virus that day. The second time Bo ran with the ball in that game, he scored a 55-yard touchdown! Bo later ran 80 yards for another score, and the Tigers beat Florida 28-21.

Bo gained 100 yards or more in 6 of his 11 games that season. The Tigers lost only once, and they became the SEC Champions for the first time since 1957.

Of course, Bo's best performance was against Alabama. The game was played on December 3, 1983, at Legion Field in Birmingham. A driving rainstorm made the field slippery on game day, but that did not bother Bo.

In the first half, Bo took a handoff and ran to his left toward a hole his blockers had made in Alabama's defensive line. Suddenly, the hole closed. Bo cut sharply back to his right toward another hole, but that one closed too. Bo then cut back to his left and ran 69 yards for a touchdown!

Auburn was leading 16-13 in the third quarter when Alabama scored a touchdown to take the lead, 20-16. Seventeen seconds after play resumed, Bo ran 71 yards for the winning touchdown. Auburn won 23-20. The Tigers had beaten Alabama for the second year in a row, and Bo had gained 256 yards rushing!

"It's like I have to pay that coach back for what he said," Bo said after the game. "That gives me incentive to play until I can't play anymore."

The Tigers were then invited to compete in the Sugar Bowl. The Sugar Bowl is played in New Orleans, Louisiana. College football holds four major "bowl" games on New Year's Day, and the Sugar Bowl is one of them. The others are the Rose Bowl, the Cotton Bowl, and the Orange Bowl.

The Tigers' opponents in the Sugar Bowl were the Michigan Wolverines, a tough defensive team that had allowed opposing teams to gain an average of only 96 yards each game that season. Bo made the Wolverine defense look like Swiss cheese when he gained 130 yards. The Tigers won 9-7, and Bo was named the Sugar Bowl MVP.

Bo's sophomore football season had been spectacular. He gained a total of 1,213 yards and he led the SEC in rushing touchdowns with 12. "Bo was far better this season than a year ago," Coach Dye said. "I've been excited about the change I've seen in him this year."

Fans and sportswriters were excited, too. Bo had won All-America and All-SEC honors. He had also gained more yards rushing than any other major college running back except Mike Rozier of Nebraska. Rozier won the Heisman Trophy that year.

Bo was pleased by what he had done that season and he was happier with the rest of his life, too. He had begun to control his stutter by teaching himself to talk to everyone the same way he talked to his friends, his family, and other people with whom he felt relaxed and comfortable. Bo spent more time with friends and he started to date women.

Bo's grades improved and he had a C+ average. He was majoring in business and minoring in child psychology. Bo especially enjoyed his child psychology courses because they gave him an opportunity to work with kids at Auburn's Child Study Center.

Bo only ran track during the spring semester that year. He quit baseball because he could not get along with his team's coach.

Bo competed in major track meets, such as the Millrose Games in New York City and the Florida Relays. He ran the 60-yard dash at the Millrose Games and almost had a chance to qualify for the 1984 Olympic Trials in the 100-yard dash. But his best time (10.39 seconds) at the Florida Relays wasn't good enough. If Bo's time had been only one-hundredth of a second faster, he could have tried out for the United States Olympic Track Team!

Bo then decided to quit track. He realized that if he wanted to be an Olympic sprinter like Carl Lewis, he would have to concentrate only on track. And he still wanted to play football.

There were rumors that Bo was going to leave Auburn that summer to play pro football for the Birmingham Stallions of the United States Football League. Robert Irsay, who owns the Indianapolis Colts of the NFL, also told reporters that he was going to offer Bo more than two million dollars to play for his team.

The rumors turned out to be false and Irsay never made the offer he had talked about. Bo wanted to stay in college, anyway, and he had been named Auburn's Male Athlete of the Year. He wanted to win the Heisman Trophy. Bo planned to do great things during his junior season with the Auburn Tigers. He did not plan, however, on how painful and frustrating that season would be.

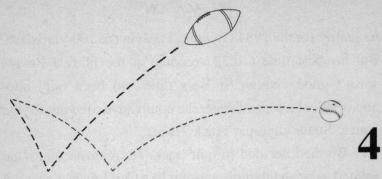

4

The Broken Dream

Auburn's fans were very excited and hopeful when the 1984 college football season began. The Tigers were favored to win the national championship, and Bo was a top contender for the Heisman Trophy. GO BO GO bumper stickers seemed to be everywhere in Auburn that fall.

Bo's chances of winning the Heisman were very good. Lionel James had left Auburn to play in the NFL and Bo was the team's top running back. Coach Dye had changed the Tiger offense so that Bo could carry the ball more often than he had during his first two seasons.

Bo tried to concentrate on learning the new plays Coach Dye had designed for him, but it was hard for him to take his mind off the Heisman Trophy. Nearly every day, reporters asked him if he thought he would win it. Whenever he walked into Jordan-Hare Stadium, Bo passed by a display case that held a replica of the famous trophy.

The Heisman Trophy was named after John Heisman, who was a college football coach from 1892 to 1927. Heisman coached at several schools, including Auburn, and he won 185 games and lost only 70 during his career.

The replica in Jordan-Hare Stadium was in honor of quarterback Pat Sullivan, who won the Heisman Trophy in 1971. Sullivan had been the last Auburn player to win it, and Bo hoped to be the next. But he said, "My main goal is to be 100 percent the player I can be. That means not only running and blocking, but catching the ball and going to team meetings. If I win the Heisman, I'll be happy. If I don't, I won't lose any sleep over it."

Auburn's fans probably lost some sleep after the Tigers were beaten 20-18 by Miami in their first game that season. Bo gained 96 yards, but he injured his ankle late in the game. He spent the next week on crutches and was unable to practice.

When the Tigers played the University of Texas Longhorns two weeks later, Bo's ankle was stiff and sore. He decided to play anyway, even though he limped when he walked and seemed to be a step or two slower when he ran.

At first, Bo's ankle did not appear to be bothering him. By the middle of the game's third quarter, he had carried the ball 13 times for 50 yards and he had scored a touchdown. Then disaster struck.

Bo took a handoff and sprinted 53 yards. He was on his way to a touchdown, but his ankle slowed him just enough for Longhorn safety Jerry Gray to catch him. Gray tackled Bo, who landed heavily on the hard AstroTurf™ field.

Bo felt a sharp pain in his right shoulder. He had to use his left arm to lift himself up off the field. Bo ran with the ball two more times, but his shoulder hurt so much that he had to leave the game. The Tigers were shaken by Bo's injury. They fumbled the ball away twice during the fourth quarter, and Texas went on to win 35-27.

Bo was taken to a hospital where doctors examined his shoulder. They told him that it had been severely separated, and that he would not be able to play for the rest of the season. "I cried like crazy," Bo said. "I had so many hopes and it was all down the drain."

Bo had never suffered a serious injury before. He felt depressed and he hated not being able to play. Luckily, the Tigers won their next six games in a row without him.

Perhaps the brightest moment in Bo's life that fall was when he met Linda Garrett. Linda was a student at Auburn. She admired Bo as an athlete, but she also liked him because he was a bright person. "I noticed that right away," Linda says. "He wasn't a dumb jock by any means."

Bo and Linda began to date. At first, Bo was so quiet that Linda wondered if he was ever going to open up. "It took him seven months to do that when we were dating at Auburn," Linda says. Bo and Linda eventually got married on September 5, 1987.

Bo's shoulder healed more quickly than the doctors had expected. He was able to play against Florida after only six weeks. Bo no longer had any chance to win the Heisman Trophy that season, but the Tigers still had a chance to win the national championship.

Coach Dye knew that his team could not afford to lose another game, but he was also afraid that Bo would hurt his shoulder again. Bo was allowed to carry the ball only five times against Florida. The Tigers were routed 24-3.

The loss to Florida was heartbreaking, but the Tigers bounced back in their next game and creamed Cincinnati, 60-0. Bo carried the ball only eight times for 57 yards in that game, but he scored three touchdowns.

When the Tigers beat Georgia 21-12 the following week, they had a chance to play in the Sugar Bowl if they could beat Alabama in the final game of the regular season.

Bo wanted to beat The Tide for the third year in a row, and he got the chance to do it late in the fourth quarter. The Tigers had the ball on The Tide's one-yard line and it was fourth down. Auburn was losing 17-15, and there were only about three minutes left to play in the game.

The Tigers could have taken the lead by kicking a field goal, but they wanted to score a touchdown instead. In the Tiger huddle, quarterback Pat Washington called for a hand-off to Bo.

Before the play began, Washington shouted an audible. "Audibles" are code words or numbers that quarterbacks use to tell their teammates that the play they called in the huddle has been changed.

Washington tried to tell Bo to run in a different direction, but the crowd was so loud that Bo did not hear the audible. Bo ran the wrong way and Washington had to hand off to Brent Fullwood instead. Fullwood was tackled for a three-yard loss. Alabama then regained the ball and the Tigers lost 17-15.

Bo was so upset after the game that he refused to talk to reporters. Coach Dye did not blame Bo for the Tiger loss. "I tell you this," Coach Dye said. "If we get in that situation again, Bo is going to get the ball every time."

Auburn finished the regular season with eight wins and four losses. Instead of a national championship and an appearance in a major bowl game, they had to settle for a game against Arkansas in the Liberty Bowl. Bo scored two touchdowns, including the game-winner, and the Tigers won 21-15. Bo was named the Liberty Bowl MVP. Compared to the Heisman Trophy, that award was only a consolation prize.

Bo made up for his disappointing football season after he rejoined Auburn's baseball team the following spring. Bo played centerfield and batted .401 with 17 home runs and 43 runs batted in.

Baseball was fun for Bo again because Auburn had a new coach named Hal Baird. Bo liked Coach Baird, and

Baird was very impressed by how good Bo was. "Bo is the best baseball player I've ever seen," Baird said. "Mickey Mantle is the closest comparison I can make."

Major league scouts agreed. "Bo has got as much talent as Mickey Mantle or Willie Mays," said Dick Egan of the Major League Scouting Bureau. "In high school, I gave Bo three eights [on a scale of two to eight] in throwing, power, and speed. You could scout for years and years and never see a guy like that."

Bo was so fast that he stole nine bases in a row before he was thrown out by a catcher that spring. One time, he hit a ball back to the pitcher on one bounce and *still* beat the pitcher's throw to first base!

Bo's power was dazzling, too. In a game against Georgia on April 2, 1985, Bo hit a 425-foot home run that was still rising when it hit an 85-foot-tall light pole behind the centerfield fence! "That was the longest home run I've ever seen an amateur player hit," said Coach Baird.

Bo also threw baseballs as well as he hit them. Scouts timed his fastball at 88 miles per hour. Most major league pitchers throw fastballs at that speed. And Bo threw his fastball without even winding up!

Coach Baird, who had played minor league baseball, said, "In seven years in pro baseball, I saw four or five guys who had the power Bo does, three or four guys who could run like he can, and three or four who could throw like he can. But those were twelve different people. It sounds like I'm talking about Superman."

Superman, however, did have a weakness: kryptonite. Bo's kryptonite was the fact that he had rarely practiced to improve his baseball skills. Bo succeeded more easily in football because he could use his size and strength when he ran with the ball. Baseball requires coordination and timing. Those things are best developed by practice.

Bo often misjudged fly balls in the outfield, and he sometimes allowed runners to score because he threw the ball to the wrong base. Bo also struck out 41 times that season.

"Bo's not really a polished player right now," Coach Baird said. "He's an unrefined talent. But he is without a doubt the finest talent I have ever seen."

Dick Egan said that Bo could be a major league team's biggest star, but only if Bo devoted himself to baseball.

Bo did not know which sport he wanted to play after

college. He loved baseball, but he didn't like the idea that he would first have to spend a year or two in the minor leagues. Football was more tempting because he could play in the NFL or the USFL right away.

Bo kept people in suspense for several weeks after his junior year at Auburn. Nearly every day, newspapers ran stories that had headlines like, "Jackson Deciding."

On June 3, 1985, Bo was chosen by the California Angels in the major league draft of college and high school players. The Angels said that they would pay Bo more money than any draft choice had ever been paid. Bo decided to stay in college instead. "I want people at Auburn to remember me by what I do my senior year," Bo said.

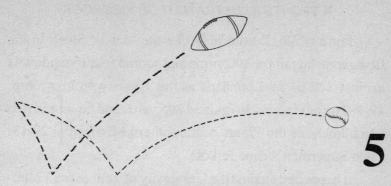

5

The Heisman Superman

It is not easy for an athlete to succeed when people expect him to be Superman. Bo was expected to be Superman during his senior year, especially after a newspaper in Atlanta, Georgia, printed a full-page picture of Bo in a Superman costume before the 1985 college football season.

Bo was favored to win the Heisman Trophy and the Tigers were favored to win the national championship. However, only one player since 1950 had won the Heisman *and* played for the national championship team during the same season. That player was running back Tony Dorsett of the University of Pittsburgh in 1976. Bo would have to play like Superman if he wanted to do what Dorsett had done.

For a while, Bo did play like the Man of Steel. In his first game, he ran for 290 yards and scored four touchdowns against Southwest Louisiana as the Tigers won in a romp, 49-7. The next week, Bo gained 205 yards and he scored two touchdowns as the Tigers beat Southern Mississippi 29-18. Then Superman's cape fell off.

It happened against the University of Tennessee Volunteers at Neyland Stadium in Knoxville, Tennessee, in front of 94,358 people. Millions of other people were watching the game on national television.

The Volunteers delighted their fans and shocked the Tigers by taking a 24-0 lead by halftime. Tennessee's defense concentrated on stopping Bo. They held him to only 80 yards rushing before they knocked him out of the game in the third quarter. As Bo sat on the bench with an ice pack on his knee, he was taunted by fans who yelled, "He's scared!" and "Bo just gave up!" Tennessee won 38-20.

Bo bounced back the next week to gain 240 yards and score two touchdowns against Mississippi as the Tigers won 41-0. Then Bo scored two touchdowns and gained 176 yards as the Tigers walloped Florida State 59-27. Against Georgia Tech, Bo gained 242 yards and scored two touchdowns in the Tigers' 17-14 win. He also gained 169 yards and scored two touchdowns against Mississippi State. The Tigers won that game 21-9.

It seemed that Superman had returned to stay, when suddenly his cape fell off again against Florida on November 2, 1985. Late in the first half, Bo was tackled hard by Florida linebacker Alonzo Johnson. Bo's thigh was bruised, and he limped off the field. Bo ran only three more times that day and Florida won 14-10. People again called him a coward.

"We knew if we hit Bo hard enough, he'd take himself out of the game," Alonzo Johnson said.

Florida linebacker Leon Pennington said, "It seems like Bo has a tendency to leave the game when the going gets tough."

The losses to Tennessee and Florida badly damaged the Tigers' chances of winning the national championship, and Bo was criticized for not trying to help his team even though he was hurt. "I thought that criticism was sickening," said Tiger running back Tim Jessie. "I had a bruised thigh, too. To me it's pretty much like a broken leg. Your leg just doesn't work."

Tiger running back Tommie Agee said, "Bo's not a

quitter. If he could go, he would play hurt."

Coach Dye said, "Bo has never displayed anything but courage."

Bo's leg still hurt when the Tigers played their next game, but he insisted on playing because the game was going to be his last at Jordan-Hare Stadium. Bo carried the ball only 14 times and gained 73 yards, but the Tigers beat East Carolina anyway, 35-10.

Bo felt better the following week. He gained 121 yards and scored two touchdowns against Georgia as the Tigers won 24-10. The Tigers then played Alabama in their final regular season game. Bo gained 142 yards and scored two touchdowns, but the Tigers lost 25-23.

Few people knew that Bo had played against Alabama even though several of his ribs were cracked. He had cracked them in the game against Georgia, but he had not told anyone except Coach Dye.

"I listened to all the criticism and I had to prove myself all over again," Bo said. "I'm not a quitter. If I felt it was necessary to take myself out of competition, it was not because I'm a coward."

Bo finished the regular season with 1,786 yards rushing

and 17 touchdowns. Those were the best totals of his college career, but it seemed possible that Bo would not win the Heisman Trophy anyway.

The Heisman is awarded to the college player who receives the most votes from sportswriters. Many sportswriters felt that Bo did not deserve to win the Heisman because he had taken himself out of the two games that had cost the Tigers the national championship.

On December 7, 1985, the winner of the Heisman Trophy was announced at the Downtown Athletic Club in New York City. Bo Jackson had won the award after the closest vote in Heisman history. He received 317 first place votes, 218 second place votes, and 122 third place votes, for a total of 1,509 points. Quarterback Chuck Long of Iowa finished second, only 45 points behind Bo.

"I thought my heart was going to jump out of my shirt when I heard the vote was that close," Bo said. "Winning the Heisman means a great deal to me."

The Heisman Trophy brought Bo more attention than ever before. He had to change his phone number three times that month. When the Tigers went to Dallas, Texas, to play in the Cotton Bowl, Bo needed bodyguards to keep reporters and fans away from him when he wanted peace and quiet.

"The way life has changed is that I can't go anywhere without people noticing me," Bo said. "Being just another Auburn student is probably the only time I can be just another face in the crowd. That's the way I like it. I like going to class. I like taking notes and asking questions and trying to learn just like anybody else, with nobody expecting me to do something great."

Reporters kept asking Bo, "What pro sport are you going to play after you graduate?" Bo often refused to say, but he did tell a reporter from *Sports Illustrated*, "I wish I could do both. At least, I'd like to try it to see if I liked it, but there's always going to be somebody who says that I can't do that."

The 1986 Cotton Bowl was Bo's final game with the Tigers. He ran for 129 yards against Texas A&M, but the Tigers lost 36-16. It was a disappointing way for Bo's football career at Auburn to end, but he had a lot to be proud of. Bo had set or tied 12 Auburn records! He had also become the school's all-time leader in yards rushing (4,303), touchdowns (43), points (274), and games with 100 or more yards rushing (21).

"Bo is unquestionably the greatest all-around athlete I have ever been around," Coach Dye said. "I can't think of anybody who was ever responsible for winning more big ballgames. Bo hasn't had to make any apologies, either. That includes when he went the wrong way and we lost to Alabama, and when he had to come out of a couple of games because he got hurt."

Winning the Heisman Trophy assured Bo that he would be drafted by an NFL team that spring. NFL scouts raved about him and said that he was the best running back to come out of college since O.J. Simpson in 1969.

People assumed that Bo would play pro football because that was what every Heisman Trophy winner since 1958 had done. Bo did not want to choose his sport until after he had played his final college baseball season, though.

Bo batted .258 with seven home runs in his first 20 games that spring. He struggled at first and struck out 30 times in his first 69 at-bats. Bo was just beginning to solve his hitting problems when he made a mistake that ended his college baseball career.

On March 25, 1986, Bo went to Tampa, Florida, to be examined by team doctors for the Tampa Bay Buccaneers.

The Buccaneers had the first pick in the NFL Draft that year, and they wanted to choose Bo. When Bo flew to Florida on the team's private plane, he broke a rule that did not allow SEC athletes to accept favors from pro teams. If they did, they could no longer play sports for their schools.

Bo said he was unaware of that rule and that he would not have gone to Tampa if he had known he would be suspended. Nevertheless, Bo was forbidden to play baseball again at Auburn. That made some major league scouts doubt that Bo would be able to play in the big leagues.

Those scouts said that Bo did not have enough experience in baseball. He had played in a total of only 89 games during his four years at Auburn. Bo's 30 strikeouts that spring had shown that he needed more practice. Some scouts even doubted that Bo was very good at baseball at all.

"Bo has got to play football," said scouting director Ben Wade of the Los Angeles Dodgers. "He's not the best prospect in the country. He has some tools, but there are a lot of kids in Class A ball with better tools than him right now." (Class A is the lowest level of minor league baseball.)

Bo had lost valuable playing time in baseball, but he did not panic. He decided to wait until after the NFL draft that April because he wanted to make the right choice. Bo talked to Coach Dye, and he met with the California Angels in Anaheim, California, the week before the NFL draft.

While he was in Anaheim, Bo met the Angels' star outfielder, Reggie Jackson. Reggie was one of Bo's idols. "We sat down and talked about life," Bo says. "He talked to me as an experienced man to a young man, and I really enjoyed my conversation."

Reggie told Bo, "I understand people think you can hit .300, get fifty home runs, and fifty-to-seventy-five stolen bases. That means you can be the best baseball player there has ever been." Bo thought more seriously about playing pro baseball after Reggie said *that*!

On April 29, 1986, Bo was the first player chosen in the NFL draft. The Buccaneers then offered him 4.6 million dollars to play for them for five years. That was more money than any NFL rookie had ever been paid. Bo told the Buccaneers that he wanted to wait until after the baseball draft in June before he would accept their offer.

Fans and sportswriters thought that Bo was wrong to wait. Most major league teams were convinced that Bo would play pro football, so they were not interested in even drafting him. Some people said Bo was waiting only because he thought the Buccaneers would offer him even more money if they thought that he would play baseball instead.

"Money can't buy happiness," Bo told reporters. "I've been poor all my life, so I can't miss something that I never had. I'm just looking forward to doing something that I like after I leave Auburn. I get the same kick from running for a touchdown as I do when I hit a home run."

A week before the baseball draft, Bo met with the Kansas City Royals. Royals general manager John Schuerholz asked Bo if he liked baseball as much as football. "I have learned to love football as much as baseball," Bo replied.

Royals scout Ken Gonzales had been watching Bo play baseball for five years and he had graded Bo's skills. Gonzales had given Bo a total grade of 71 points. Most superstars get grades of 70 points. The Major League Scouting Bureau had given Bo a total grade of 75.5 points!

On June 2, 1986, the Royals gambled that Bo would choose to play baseball and they made him the 105th player chosen in the draft. Bo then kept the world of sports waiting in suspense for another three weeks.

Finally, on June 21, 1986, Bo announced at a press conference that he had agreed to play for the Royals. "I went with what is in my heart," Bo told reporters that day. "My first love is baseball and it has always been a dream to be a major league player. My goal now is to be the best baseball player that Bo Jackson can be."

Bo's announcement stunned many people, especially when they learned that the Royals were going to pay him about one million dollars to play for them for three years. That was a lot of money, but it was still about three million dollars less than the Buccaneers had offered to pay him. Star athletes almost always accept contracts that pay them the most money. Bo had not done that.

"I'm always going to do the opposite of what the public thinks," Bo said. "I did this so people would swallow their Adam's apples."

After the press conference, Bo flew to Kansas City. He went to Royals Stadium, borrowed a pair of cleats, a glove, and a bat, and then he went out to the field.

Several Royals players gathered around the batting practice cage to watch Bo hit. Bo hit the first pitch more than 410 feet! The ball sailed over the leftfield fence and landed on a grass embankment. He hit the next pitch more than 450 feet over the centerfield fence!

Royals second baseman Frank White shook his head in wonder and said, "I've never seen a ball hit that far in this park."

Hal McRae, the Royals designated hitter, said, "He didn't even hit them good and they still went out. He has a nice smooth swing. He reminds me of Reggie Jackson."

Dick Howser, who was the manager of the Royals at the time, said, "I've never seen anybody with the batting strength this kid has. For sheer power, he's like Mickey Mantle, Harmon Killebrew, and Frank Howard were. He's like Jose Canseco is now."

Bo worked out with the Royals for the next 10 days. John Schuerholz knew that Bo was not ready to play in the major leagues, but he wanted to decide if Bo should be sent to the Royals' Triple A minor league team in Omaha, Nebraska, or their Double A team in Memphis, Tennessee.

Schuerholz decided that Bo would improve more quickly by playing in a Double A league. Bo was then sent to Memphis. He was told that if he played well there, it was possible that he could join the Royals that September.

Bo did not mind being sent to the minor leagues. "I'm so happy right now, I wouldn't care if they sent me down to Pee Wee ball," he said.

Bo's attitude pleased the Royals. "There are two things a scout never knows for sure," said Ken Gonzales. "They are whether a guy's talent has peaked and how badly he wants to reach the majors. There's no doubt about how badly Bo wants to make it, and he certainly hasn't begun to reach his peak. To me, he's one in a million both on and off the field. The people of Kansas City are going to be fortunate to see this young man play."

Bo was excited about his new career. "I'm ready to go to work," he said. "I don't have a timetable for when I might move up to the Royals, but let me state a fact: Bo Jackson can play baseball."

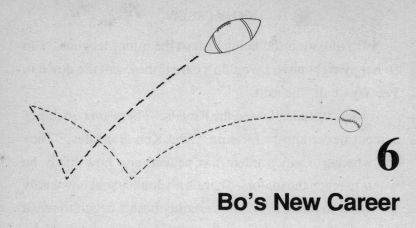

6

Bo's New Career

Bo joined the Memphis Chicks of the Southern League on June 27, 1986. A crowd of reporters was waiting for him when he arrived at McCarver Stadium in Memphis, Tennessee. The city was buzzing with excitement about the college football superstar who had come to town to play baseball, so Bo's teammates poked fun at him by wearing Buccaneer jerseys.

When Bo went out to the field, players stopped warming up so they could watch him take batting practice. The Chicks pitching coach, Rich Dubee, threw 23 pitches and Bo hit 9 of them over the fence!

"It's kind of scary to see the way the ball jumps off his

Bo, playing for Auburn, soared over the Michigan Wolverines defense at the 1984 Sugar Bowl in New Orleans, Louisiana. He led the Tigers to a 9-7 victory, gaining 130 yards and earning himself MVP honors.

Not many people know that Bo Jackson ran track while he was in college — or that he was good enough to win the open 100-meter race at the 1984 Florida Sunkist Relay at Pearcy Beard Track in Gainsville, Florida (above). Fewer people know how much of a family man Bo is now. He spends his free time with his wife, Linda, and their three children, Morgan, Garrett and Nicholas. He also keeps in touch with his mother, Florence, and his brothers and sisters— all nine of them (right).

Joe McNally / Sports Illustrated

Playing centerfield for Auburn during his junior year, Bo batted .401 with 17 home runs and 43 RBIs. That same season, he struck out 41 times. It was no wonder that Auburn baseball coach Hal Baird described him as an unrefined talent.

Amazing Fact

Bo is so strong that he once snapped a baseball bat in half over his knee after he struck out in a game against the Cleveland Indians!

Bo was awarded the Heisman Trophy on December 7, 1985 at the Downtown Athletic Club in New York City. He beat out Iowa quarterback Chuck Long by only 45 points, the closest vote in Heisman history. Chuck now plays for the Detroit Lions.

Bo once threw a baseball from the foot of the outfield wall all the way to home plate — about 300 feet — to catch Harold Reynolds, the Seattle Mariners' fastest runner, and end the inning. Bo's ability to field his position has been described as superhuman.

Bo played his first game for the Raiders on October 25, 1987, against the New England Patriots in Foxboro, Massachusetts. The Pats beat the Raiders, but Bo carried the ball eight times and gained 37 yards. He was happy with his performance in his NFL debut — and so were the Raiders.

Amazing Fact

Bo's chest measures 48 inches. His waist measures 35 inches. Each of his thighs measures 39 inches. Is each of your thighs thicker than your waist?

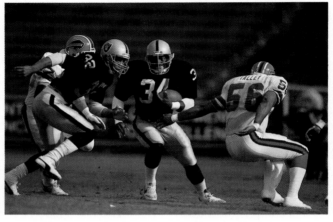

People wondered what would happen between Bo and Marcus Allen, one of the best halfbacks in the NFL, when Bo joined the Raiders. Knowing that Bo could be a big help to the team, Marcus offered to move to fullback and the two became friends. When Bo ran the ball, Marcus blocked for him.

Who had the longest run for a touchdown?

A. Tony Dorsett of the Dallas Cowboys
B. Bo Jackson of the Los Angeles Raiders
C. Walter Payton of the Chicago Bears.

A. Tony Dorsett, 99 yards.

Bo played baseball well in 1988 until he tore a hamstring in his left leg. After he returned from his injury, he batted only .205 in his final 78 games. Fans and reporters accused him of playing badly because he had pigskin (football) on the brain.

Amazing Fact

Bo is a right-handed batter who can run from home plate to first base (90 feet) in 3.6 seconds. The fastest left-handed batters run that distance in 3.8 seconds. Bo must run an extra step because he has to step over home plate to get to first and lefties don't have to.

In one of his best games of the 1988 football season, Bo (above, in black) showed how effective a receiver he could be in a game against the Denver Broncos on December 4. He caught six passes, gaining 138 yards. The 21-20 win put the Raiders in first place in their division, but they didn't hold on long enough to make the playoffs.

Longest Runs In NFL History

Yardage	Player(s)
99	Tony Dorsett
97	Andy Uram, Bob Gage
96	Jim Spavital, Bob Hoernschemeyer
94	O. J. Simpson
92	Kenny Washingon, Bo Jackson

In the 1989 All-Star Game in Anaheim, California, Bo made a running catch in leftfield to prevent the National League from breaking the game open in the first inning. He followed it up, as the first American League player to bat, with a home run.

All-Star Game MVPs 1986-1990

Year	Player
1986	Roger Clemens, Boston, P
1987	Tim Raines, Montral, C
1988	Terry Steinbach, Oakland, C
1989	Bo Jackson, Kansas City, LF
1990	Julio Franco, Texas, 2B

On July 10, 1989, Bo became the first player since Willie Mays to hit a home run and steal a base in the same All-Star Game. He also made several good defensive plays and had two runs batted in. He was named the All-Star Game's Most Valuable Player.

BO JACKSON...HAS

ALWAYS BEEN A FANTASTIC ATHLETE. BUT IT WAS NOT EASY TO CONVINCE PEOPLE THAT HE COULD PLAY TWO PROFESSIONAL SPORTS IN THE SAME YEAR. THEY WOULD EVENTUALLY LEARN THAT BO COULD BE A SUPERSTAR IN BOTH BASEBALL AND FOOTBALL!

WHEN BO WAS YOUNG, HE WAS KNOWN AS THE BULLY IN THE NEIGHBORHOOD. HE WOULD CAUSE TROUBLE AND KIDS WERE AFRAID OF HIM.

WATCH OUT! HERE COMES BO! LET'S GET OUTTA' HERE!

I'M RIGHT BEHIND YOU!

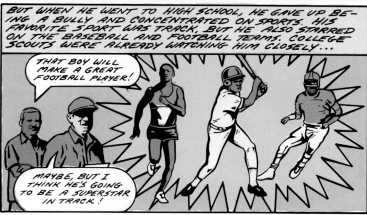

BUT WHEN HE WENT TO HIGH SCHOOL, HE GAVE UP BEING A BULLY AND CONCENTRATED ON SPORTS. HIS FAVORITE SPORT WAS TRACK, BUT HE ALSO STARRED ON THE BASEBALL AND FOOTBALL TEAMS. COLLEGE SCOUTS WERE ALREADY WATCHING HIM CLOSELY...

THAT BOY WILL MAKE A GREAT FOOTBALL PLAYER!

MAYBE, BUT I THINK HE'S GOING TO BE A SUPERSTAR IN TRACK!

BEING A COLLEGE STAR WASN'T ALWAYS EASY FOR BO. FOR ONE THING, FOOTBALL PRACTICE WAS A LOT TOUGHER THAN IT HAD BEEN IN HIGH SCHOOL. AND BO, WHO HAD NEVER BEEN AWAY FROM HOME, GOT SO HOMESICK, HE SPENT 6 HOURS IN A BUS STATION DECIDING WHETHER HE SHOULD LEAVE SCHOOL!

BUT BO STAYED IN SCHOOL AND CONTINUED TO PLAY FOOTBALL. IN 1985, HIS PATIENCE AND HARD WORK PAID OFF. HE WON THE HEISMAN TROPHY—THE AWARD FOR THE BEST COLLEGE FOOTBALL PLAYER IN THE COUNTRY!

WHAT CAN YOU SAY ABOUT BO, COACH?

ONLY THAT HE'S THE BEST FOOTBALL PLAYER I'VE EVER SEEN!

IN 1986, BO SHOCKED EVERYONE BY SIGNING A CONTRACT TO PLAY PROFESSIONAL BASEBALL WITH THE KANSAS CITY ROYALS. EVERYONE THOUGHT HE WOULD PLAY FOOTBALL FOR THE TAMPA BAY BUCCANEERS WHO HAD DRAFTED HIM, BUT IT WAS BASEBALL THAT BO TRULY LOVED!

I CAN'T BELIEVE IT! HE'S MAKING A BIG MISTAKE!

HE SURE IS! HE'S THROWING HIS FOOTBALL CAREER RIGHT OUT THE WINDOW!

BUT BO WASN'T MAKING A MISTAKE. IN HIS FIRST GAME FOR THE ROYALS, HE HIT A GROUND BALL TO THE INFIELD. THANKS TO HIS SPEED, HE MADE IT TO FIRST BASE SAFELY, FOR HIS FIRST MAJOR LEAGUE HIT!

THAT KID'S SURE GOT SOME SPEED!

YEAH, HE'S GOING TO BE GOOD FOR THIS CLUB!

BUT IT WASN'T SMOOTH SAILING FROM THERE. IN 1987, BO SIGNED A FOOTBALL CONTRACT WITH THE RAIDERS. ROYALS FANS WERE VERY ANGRY WITH BO. AT THE NEXT GAME, THEY THREW PLASTIC FOOTBALLS AT HIM!

HEY BO! YOU'RE ON THE WRONG FIELD, YOU *TRAITOR!*

GO HOME BO!

BO SHOWED THE WORLD HE COULD STILL PLAY FOOTBALL. IN A GAME AGAINST THE SEATTLE SEAHAWKS, SHOWN ON NATIONAL TV, BO RUSHED FOR 221 YARDS. HE ALSO RAN OVER BRIAN BOSWORTH FOR ONE OF HIS TWO TOUCHDOWNS!

OUR BO IS BACK!

YES SIR, HE'S STILL AWESOME!

bat," Dubee said. "They say he's awesome, and he is."

Tommy Jones, the Chicks manager, said, "I swear I'm looking at Ted Williams!"

Bo did not play that night because Jones wanted to give him time to get ready. Bo spent the next two days taking batting practice and shagging (catching) fly balls in the outfield.

Bo played for the Chicks against the Columbus (Georgia) Astros on June 30, 1986. A crowd of 7,026 fans, including Bo's mother, went to McCarver Stadium to see the game that night. Usually, the Chicks drew crowds of about 3,000 people! Nearly 150 reporters were there, too.

Bo was given a standing ovation when he went to bat for the first time in the game. The crowd chanted, "Bo! Bo! Bo!" and he replied by hitting a sharp single into centerfield to drive in a run. Bo later grounded out to the pitcher and he struck out twice. The Chicks lost 9-5, but Bo enjoyed his first game anyway.

"I'm satisfied," he said after the game. "I don't want to judge how I did. I'm just happy to be playing baseball."

Reporters wanted to know if Bo got along with his new teammates. "Everybody gets along with him," Tommy

Jones said. "Nobody is treating him differently than any other player or making him out to be Superman."

That was good for Bo because he played like Clark Kent after that. He failed to get a hit in six of his next eight games, and he got only four hits in his first 45 at-bats. Bo also made two errors.

Bo's poor performance made people wonder if he had made a mistake by trying to play pro baseball. Sportswriter Bernard Fernandez of *The Philadelphia Daily News* wrote, "Is the most celebrated minor leaguer in history the real thing, or is he simply a great football player disguising himself in the wrong sports uniform?"

Bo quickly became tired of hearing people say that. "Every day people are telling me that I should have played pro football," Bo said. "I just tell them to sit back on their cans and watch. Nothing makes me feel better than making somebody wrong."

Tommy Jones defended Bo by explaining, "He has very little experience. You can have incredible instincts as Bo does, but they don't surface until you have a chance to play over and over in games."

Other players in the Southern League agreed. "Right

now, Bo is overmatched in this league," said pitcher Mitch Cook of the Columbus Astros. "The ability is there, but he's not ready for Double A ball."

Cook's teammate, pitcher Anthony Kelley, said, "I struck Bo out twice. There were some pitches he couldn't do anything about. He'll get with it after some work."

No one had to tell Bo that it would only be a matter of time until he played as well as he was expected to. "When I break the ice, I'm going to break it big," Bo promised.

Bo kept his promise. During a period of eight games in the middle of July, Bo got 11 hits in 26 at-bats. He also hit two home runs, including a 554-foot grand slam. A "grand slam" is a home run with three runners on base. Bo was then named the Southern League Player of the Week.

By August, Bo was batting .262, and he had six home runs and 21 runs batted in. He had not played like a superstar since he had also struck out 53 times and made six errors, but he was improving.

"Bo improves every time he goes out on the field," Tommy Jones said. "He has been able to take coaching directions and apply them in games that very night."

No matter how well Bo played, people still said that he

would return to football because he had learned that he could not become a baseball star instantly. Fans in Charlotte, North Carolina, threw plastic footballs at Bo during a game that summer. Chicks shortstop Joe Jarrell told reporters that he had seen Bo watching an NFL preseason game on TV. "He was really getting into it," Jarrell said. "I told him he better stay away from football or he'll start missing it."

When Bo was asked, for perhaps the millionth time, if he missed football, he said, "There is nothing about football that I really miss. I don't know why that's so hard for everybody to understand. For the last six years, it was a part of my life and I enjoyed every minute of it. Now I'm strictly a baseball player."

The rumors about Bo leaving baseball stopped for a while after he joined the Royals on September 1, 1986. In 53 games with the Chicks, Bo had batted .277 with seven home runs and 25 runs batted in. John Schuerholz then wanted to see Bo test himself in the big leagues.

Bo's first test was against the Chicago White Sox at Royals Stadium on September 2, 1986. In the second inning, Bo went to bat against pitcher Steve Carlton. Steve had won the Cy Young Award four times during his career. The Cy

Young Award is given each year to the best pitcher in the American League and the National League.

Carlton was nearing the end of his career at that time and he was no longer a great pitcher, but it was a fitting matchup: a pitcher who would certainly be elected to the Hall of Fame versus a young rookie who might one day be a Hall of Famer, too.

Bo hit one of Carlton's pitches 425 feet, but the ball landed in foul territory. Bo then hit a ground ball to the second baseman and safely beat the throw to first base. He had gotten a hit in his first major league at-bat!

Bo grounded out in his next two at-bats, though. His major league debut had not been spectacular, but it had been memorable. "Bo can say that he got his first hit off a Hall of Famer and be proud of that," said Royals manager Mike Ferraro.

"I did not expect to do something spectacular," Bo said. "I just went out and played ball."

Bo did more than just play ball during his next five games. He batted .400! Then, on September 14, 1986, Bo did something spectacular: he hit a 475-foot home run off pitcher Mike Moore of the Seattle Mariners. Bo's blast was the longest home run ever hit at Royals Stadium!

After the game, reporters asked Bo if his home run had been a thrill. "Yes and no," Bo replied. "It was my first home run in the majors, but I was concentrating at the time on helping us win the game. Now I look at it as just another hit."

That night, TV sportscasters all over the country showed Bo's "just another hit" on their highlight films. Reggie Jackson saw the replay of the home run, and he demanded to speak to Bo before the Angels played the Royals a few days later.

"Where is he?" Reggie yelled from the Angels dugout during the pregame warm-ups. "He hits one home run and he's famous! He's a superstar already! Where is he?"

Bo came out of the Royals dugout and he had a friendly chat with Reggie. Bo later showed his idol what he could do in person by hitting a game-tying home run in the eighth inning!

There were also times when Bo's poor performance at bat and in the field wound up on sports lowlight films. He struck out 34 times in his 82 at-bats with the Royals that September. In the final game of the season, he misjudged a fly ball in leftfield and crashed into the fence. The ball proceeded to land right next to him on the field.

In all, Bo batted .207 with two home runs and nine runs batted in during his introduction to major league baseball. "He's been everything we expected and he's done some things that were absolutely eye-opening," said John Schuerholz. Mike Ferraro said, "I hope to be around to see what he is like in three years."

As for Bo, his first year in pro baseball had been a wonderful experience. "I thought playing baseball would be great, but it's been even better than I thought," he said. "I'm very happy that I have accomplished the things I have so far. I'm still learning, but right now I can say I'm enjoying the heck out of myself."

Reporters asked Bo if he expected to start his next season in the minor leagues. Bo's reply was, "I promised myself that when I got to the majors, I was going to stay there."

John Schuerholz was asked the same question. "Bo could very well be with our club next season. It would not be surprising to us. Maybe he doesn't always make contact with the ball, but he will. When he does, watch out! People will be talking a long time about his accomplishments."

Schuerholz was right, but the accomplishments that people would talk about were not the ones that he had in mind when he said that.

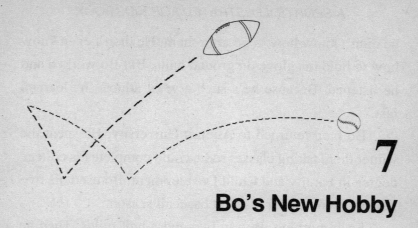

7

Bo's New Hobby

Bo learned a very important lesson during his first season in pro baseball: becoming a major league star requires hard work, practice, and, most of all, time. So after the 1986 major league season ended, Bo went to Sarasota, Florida, to play in the Instructional League.

The Instructional League is where young players practice the skills they need to play in the majors. Bo spent the rest of that October and the first week of November working on hitting and fielding.

"Bo worked his tail off," said Ed Napoleon, who was Bo's instructor. "I hit balls that I knew he couldn't get to, and he would go after them as hard as he could, even though he didn't know how to go after them. He didn't even know how to hold his glove on ground balls. But Bo worked and he listened. Because he's such a great athlete, he learned fast."

Bo then returned to Auburn University. He spent the winter there taking classes so he could complete his college degree in Family and Child Development. Bo used his free time to get ready for his next baseball season.

Each morning, Bo ran two-and-a-half miles. Then he went home, took a shower, and went to class from 9 o'clock until 11. After class, Bo worked out with the Auburn baseball team until 3 o'clock in the afternoon.

Coach Baird noticed right away that something was different about Bo. "I was astounded," Coach Baird said. "I saw that Bo had completely committed himself to baseball greatness."

Bo told reporters that he was not interested in playing football again. "I dedicated my work habits to baseball this year," he said. "I eat and sleep baseball. Last fall, I could have gone to watch Auburn's last four football games, but I went hunting or shopping instead."

Bo's new work habits paid off during the Royals'

spring training games in March. He batted .273 with three home runs, and he led the Royals with 11 runs batted in.

John Schuerholz was impressed by Bo's progress, but he did not like Bo's 24 strikeouts in 66 at-bats that spring. Schuerholz decided that Bo should spend the first six weeks of the season in the minor leagues with the Omaha Royals.

Three days before the 1987 major league season began, Royals owner Avron Fogelman asked Schuerholz to change his mind. Fogelman said that Bo's confidence might be hurt if he was sent to the minors. Schuerholz agreed and told Bo that he had made the Royals.

Bo was happy and so were his teammates. "He deserves it," said third baseman George Brett. "There was a whole clubhouse full of guys pulling for him to make the club. I think deep inside, Bo knew he belonged here."

Some sportswriters said that the Royals did not send Bo to the minors only because they were afraid that he would quit baseball if they did. "That never entered my thinking," Fogelman said. "Bo has totally convinced me that he is not thinking about football. I may be totally wrong, but I don't think football is one of his options."

Fogelman later found out that he *was* totally wrong, but

in the meantime, Bo got off to a hot start that season. In his first eight games, Bo batted .452, hit three home runs, and he led the American League with 13 runs batted in.

On April 10, 1987, Bo got four hits in five times at-bat and drove in three runs against the New York Yankees. He also scored a run by dashing around the bases from first to home plate. "Did you see him?" Hal McRae asked reporters after the game. "Bo has to be the fastest player in the major leagues."

Bo quickly won the hearts of the fans in Kansas City. They chanted "Bo! Bo! Bo!" whenever he went to bat, and they named a section of the leftfield stands in Royals Stadium, "Bo's Leftfield Lounge."

"I hope they aren't spoiled," Bo said. "I hope they see me as a baseball player, not Superman. I expect to contribute to the team, but I'm not a one-man show."

Sometimes Bo *was* a one-man show, though. When the Royals were beaten 15-2 by the Yankees at Royals Stadium on April 11, Yankee pitcher Dennis Rasmussen knocked Bo down with a pitch in the eighth inning. Bo then got up and hit Rasmussen's next pitch over the leftfield wall!

On April 14, in a game against the Detroit Tigers at

Tiger Stadium, Bo tied a Royals' team record by driving in seven runs! He hit two home runs in that game, including a grand slam that traveled more than 410 feet!

Bo's great start showed him what he could achieve through practice and experience. "I'm getting used to seeing pitchers I haven't faced before, and I'm studying what they are throwing," he said. "I'm having the time of my life. The more I play, the better I'll get."

The Royals were impressed by Bo's new willingness to work hard. Bo no longer sat on the bench during pregame warm-ups as he had the year before. He even showed up early for batting practice every day.

"He's worked hard," said Royals manager Billy Gardner. "He came to spring training with the attitude that he wasn't going to take anything for granted. I know it's early, but you've got to like what you see in the kid."

Sometimes what people saw in the kid was the old Bo. On April 18, against the New York Yankees, Bo tied a major league record by striking out five times in one game! Sometimes, they saw the new Bo. During the first month of the season, Bo batted .324 with four home runs and 15 runs batted in.

Still, many people wondered whether Bo would play football again. Bo's agent had said that there was "absolutely no chance" that Bo would ever play in the NFL. However, Bo told sportswriter Peter Alfano of *The New York Times* that he was intrigued by the idea of playing both pro baseball and pro football.

Would Bo play football again? Reporters wanted to know the answer, so they mobbed Bo nearly every day. That made some of his teammates unhappy. They felt that Bo was getting too much attention.

One day, before a game, a group of reporters gathered around Bo in the Royals locker room. Pitcher Bret Saberhagen looked up from a card game he was playing and said, "Why don't you guys go talk to Kevin Seitzer?" Seitzer was a rookie third baseman who was batting .412 for the Royals.

After Kansas City was shut out 8-0 by the Boston Red Sox on April 21, reporters asked Royals outfielder Danny Tartabull about the game. "Go talk to Bo," Tartabull snapped. "He'll tell you everything. Now get out of here!"

Bo kept insisting that he wanted to play only baseball, but reporters kept asking him about football, especially after Bo was chosen by the Los Angeles Raiders in the NFL draft on April 28, 1987. The Raiders were able to draft Bo because he had not signed a contract with the Buccaneers within the one year time limit imposed by the NFL.

"Bo is a unique athlete," said Tom Flores, who was the head coach of the Raiders. "We realize he has a commitment to baseball, but we also feel that he can meet that commitment and still possibly help us."

Bo was asked so often if he wanted to play for the Raiders that he refused to talk about football with reporters. Bo even put a sign over his locker that read, "Don't be stupid and ask me football questions."

After that, Bo went into a slump. His batting average dropped to .264 after he struck out 20 times and got only six hits in 42 at-bats. It began to seem that Bo would break the major league record for most strikeouts in one season by a rookie, which was 185.

Bo's slump made him think seriously about football again. Then Raiders owner Al Davis called him. "Bo," Davis said, "we know you are planning to play baseball for a while. But after the baseball season is over, why don't you play football for us?"

On July 14, 1987, Bo announced that he had accepted

an offer of $7.4 million to play for the Raiders for five years. "I don't have anything to prove; I'm doing this because it is a goal," Bo told reporters that day. "I expect to play both baseball and football for several years. This chance will come along only once, and I want to go after it."

Bo then set off a firestorm of criticism when he said, "Anything I do after the baseball season is a hobby, like hunting or fishing." Bo's remark caused people to say many nasty things about him:

• **Bo cares more about money than he does about his teammates:** "Yet another dollar sign has been tacked atop the baseball standings," sportswriter Michael Madden wrote in *The Boston Globe*. "Jackson is simply thinking of himself and forgetting that his teammates are only a game or two behind the Minnesota Twins in the Western Division pennant race. And so he will become half a football player and half a baseball player, and he says that football is only a hobby."

• **Bo is conceited:** "By also playing pro football, Bo Jackson is asking to be hailed as a sports Superman," sportswriter Dave Anderson wrote in *The New York Times.*

• **Bo is a traitor:** Fans in Kansas City were upset because

Bo had agreed to play for the Raiders, who were the bitter rivals of the Kansas City Chiefs. When Bo played in his first game at Royals Stadium after his announcement, fans booed and threw plastic footballs at him. IT'S A HOBBY was printed on each football.

Bo's teammates were stunned because he had convinced them that he wanted to play only baseball. "I guess he got the last laugh, didn't he?" said outfielder Willie Wilson. "He made us believe him and now we're fools."

Royals outfielder Danny Tartabull said, "This is going to destroy the team. Everybody's upset."

Bo's teammates were angry because pro teams rarely allow players to play other sports, even for fun, because they might get injured. Yet the Royals had said that they would not try to stop Bo from playing a rough sport in a professional league.

"How can you have [New York Giants linebacker] Lawrence Taylor running into you as a hobby?" Willie Wilson asked. "Do you think Lawrence Taylor is going to think it's a hobby? It's like Bo is bigger than the Royals. They treat him like a god. I'm so mad, I can't stand it."

Royals third baseman George Brett joked, "Maybe I

can go bull-riding now, or take up sword fighting."

When Bo went into the Royals locker room after his announcement, he saw that the sign above his locker had been changed. The new sign read, "Don't be stupid and ask me baseball questions." When Bo looked up, he saw his teammates staring at him angrily.

Bo's "football is a hobby" remark also insulted his new Raider teammates. Linebacker Matt Millen said, "If Bo's not for real, the guys on this team will abuse him."

Players on other NFL teams said that they would abuse Bo too. Defensive tackle Darryl Grant of the Washington Redskins said, "I'll put a good lick on him and we'll see how he likes his new hobby."

The whole world seemed to be angry at Bo Jackson that summer, and there was more pressure on him than ever before. "Bo has opened himself up to criticism if he plays poorly," George Brett said. "People will say he's thinking about football."

That is exactly what happened. From the beginning of August until the end of that season, Bo got only nine hits and he struck out 46 times in 37 games. "He must be thinking about football plays instead of curveballs," said the general manager of another major league team.

Bo also played poorly in the outfield. He made errors that cost the Royals games against the Baltimore Orioles and the New York Yankees. In a game against the Boston Red Sox, Bo made two poor plays and was told by Royals pitcher Charlie Leibrandt, "This is the major leagues, not Little League!"

Bo's teammates complained about him so much that Royals general manager John Schuerholz called a team meeting. "I tried to get the guys off Jackson's back," Schuerholz says. "Bo thanked me for defending him and he told me he was hurt by the way some of his teammates had turned against him."

Bo continued to play so poorly that he was benched for 10 days in August. He returned to play in two games against the Texas Rangers, but he struck out six times in seven at-bats. In the second game, Bo misjudged a fly ball that allowed Texas to tie the score. The Royals later lost 3-1. Life was certainly bleak for Bo, but he said, "I'm not going to let it bother me. I'm a man of confidence."

The Royals finished in second place with a record of 83 wins and 79 losses that season. Bo had batted .235 with

22 home runs, 53 runs batted in, 10 stolen bases, and 158 strikeouts in 396 at-bats.

Bo's season had begun with cheers and the possibility that he would win the American League Rookie of the Year Award. It ended with boos, criticism, and blame from his teammates. "He was a major distraction that just ruined our season," Danny Tartabull said.

Even John Schuerholz was upset. "Bo Jackson is not one of my favorite topics," he said. "Bo stopped dead as a baseball player. I should have sent him to Triple A in July, but I didn't know if that would be fair to him or our team. I would have shipped him out if I had known that all the jealousy on the team wouldn't go away."

Reporters asked Bo how he felt. "I'll be honest with you," he said. "There were times when I was bitter. There were days when I just didn't want to come to the ballpark, and days when I couldn't wait to leave. Right now, I really can't wait to get back home."

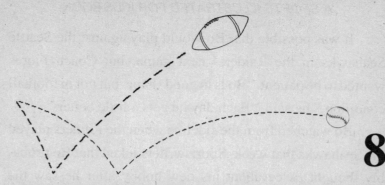

8

The Tip of the Bo Jackson Iceberg

Bo did not have to report to the Raiders until 10 days after the baseball season, so he went home to Alabama and rested.

On October 17, 1987, Bo went to El Segundo, California, and he practiced with the Raiders that day for the first time. During that practice, Bo took a handoff and then he cut upfield. Suddenly, he lost his balance and slid along the ground. Matt Millen then ran over to Bo and pretended to be an umpire.

"Safe!" Millen yelled. The other Raiders laughed and Bo tapped Millen's helmet with the football to show him that he didn't mind the joke.

It was possible that Bo would play against the Seattle Seahawks in the Raiders' next game, but Coach Flores wanted to be patient. "Bo is in good shape, but not in football condition," he said. "Each day he gets a little better."

Bo watched from the sideline when the Raiders played the Seahawks that week. Sportswriters joked that Bo probably thought twice about his new hobby after he saw the Raiders lose 35-13.

"If he got a good look at the Seahawks pounding his Raiders, Bo by now has packed his bags and headed on to try his luck on the Pro Golfers Association Tour or the tennis circuit," Scott Ostler wrote in *The Los Angeles Times*.

Bo made his NFL debut on Sunday, November 1, 1987, against the New England Patriots in Foxboro, Massachusetts. Bo did not enter the game until late in the second quarter, but he gained 14 yards the first time he carried the ball! Patriot defensive end Ken Sims hit Bo with a bone-crunching tackle, but Bo got up quickly and trotted back to the huddle.

Bo carried the ball eight times and gained 37 yards that day. "It was nothing special, nothing spectacular," Bo said after the game. "I wouldn't say I was as sharp as I was in college, but I'm happy. It's fun to be playing any sport on a professional level."

Bo saw more action against the Minnesota Vikings the next week. He carried the ball 12 times and gained 74 yards. Bo played well until the fourth quarter, when he fumbled the ball while the Raiders were trying to narrow the Vikings' 24-13 lead. Minnesota recovered Bo's fumble and scored a touchdown a few minutes later to clinch a 31-20 victory.

Bo was not in a good mood after the game. He felt that his fumble had caused the Raiders to lose their fifth game in a row. The Vikings, however, had seen how quickly Bo's rushing skills were returning.

"We barely tripped him up by the ankles," said Viking linebacker Chris Martin. "Once he gets his timing down, he'll be one heck of a running back."

Martin also told reporters that some of his friends on the Raiders had said that they resented Bo because he had joined their team in the middle of the season. If Bo had been with the Raiders since training camp, they said, he would have been able to play well right away.

Actually, Bo had been accepted by his teammates much more quickly than people knew. Bo's "football is a hobby" remark was forgotten when the other Raiders saw that he practiced hard and wanted to help the team. "I told them that I wanted to be treated like other players," Bo said.

People were especially surprised to learn that Bo got along well with Marcus Allen. Allen had been the Raiders' star running back since 1982, and he had played in four NFL Pro Bowls. (The Pro Bowl is the NFL All-Star Game.) In 1984, Allen had led the Raiders to victory in the Super Bowl and he was named that game's MVP.

Allen was a proud, cocky man, so people expected him to be angry about having to share the spotlight with Bo. Instead, Allen told Coach Flores that he wanted to do whatever he could to help Bo fit in.

"I could see that Bo could help this team," Allen said. "The season wasn't going well and we needed to make some changes to help us win. So I went to the coaches and suggested that I move to fullback so we could get Bo in the game."

There are two running backs on a football team: a fullback and a halfback. The fullback runs with the ball or blocks for the halfback. The halfback runs with the ball and also catches passes. Allen was one of the best halfbacks in the NFL, so his offer to move to fullback showed that he cared more about helping the Raiders win than he did about personal gain.

Bo felt the same way. "I don't see myself competing with Marcus," Bo said. "I see myself combining my talents with his to help the Raiders. When Marcus is running with the ball, I do my best to block. The same goes for Marcus when I've got the ball."

Allen's friendship helped Bo quickly become a better NFL player. Before the Raiders played the Denver Broncos on November 22, 1987, Allen told Bo to stop thinking so much and "to just go out there and run over people." Bo followed Allen's advice.

In the second quarter, the Raiders had the ball on the Bronco 35-yard line. Bo got the ball, faked to his right, and then ran left. Bronco defensive back Mike Harden ran up to make the tackle, but Bo put his head down and drove his helmet into Harden's chest. Harden was knocked backward as though he had been hit by a truck! Bo kept running and dove over three Broncos to score his first NFL touchdown!

"That play showed everyone what Bo can do," said Raider defensive end Howie Long. Mike Harden added,

"That's what we call a knockout play. I was a little embarrassed when I saw the replay of it on the scoreboard. That's never happened to me before."

Even though the Raiders lost that game 23-17, Bo had looked right at home in the NFL. Two weeks later, on his 25th birthday, Bo threw a party in his new home.

The party was held on Monday night, November 30, 1987, in the Seattle Kingdome. A crowd of 62,802 fans were there, and millions of others watched the game on Monday Night Football on TV. Bo ran wild, and he gained 197 yards on his first 11 carries.

In the second quarter, Bo caught a 14-yard pass for a touchdown. A few minutes later, he dashed 91 yards for another touchdown! Bo then tossed the football in the air and pretended to swing at it with a bat.

Bo partied through the third quarter and scored a two-yard touchdown by carrying Seahawk linebacker Brian Bosworth on his back into the end zone. "He just flat-out ran my butt over," Bosworth said. "My hat's off to him."

In all, Bo's birthday presents were a Raider team record of 221 yards rushing, a 37-14 victory, and NFL stardom. After Bo's spectacular game many people began to wonder why he would ever want to play baseball again.

"I hadn't thought about that," Bo said later. "Why should I? It's my birthday and I had a great time. If I do good in both sports, or do bad in one and handle the other one well, that's fine. But I'm not going to go down without a fight. I've set high goals for myself and I plan to reach them."

After Bo's birthday bash, fans in Los Angeles recognized him wherever he went. One day, Bo and Linda were shopping in Beverly Hills, which is the home of many famous movie and TV stars. People there kept walking up to Bo to shake his hand and ask for his autograph.

"My wife was so excited," Bo says. "We had lunch in a restaurant and we couldn't eat because people were walking over and asking me to sign their napkins. It's funny how a guy like me, who comes from a small town in the South, can come out here where there are thousands of famous people and all these people recognize *me*."

Fans in Kansas City recognized Bo too, but their reaction was very different. When the Raiders played the Kansas City Chiefs on December 13, 1987, Bo was booed loudly by the crowd of 63,834 people in Arrowhead Stadium. There were nasty banners in the stands. One read L.A. HAS B.O., and another read THE CHIEFS WILL TEACH BO WHAT THE ROYALS COULDN'T: HOW TO HIT!

The boos and banners did not bother Bo as much as what happened to him in that game. He carried the ball three times before he twisted his ankle. As Bo left the field to have his ankle X-rayed, fans threw baseballs at him.

Bo's ankle was not broken, but he was able to carry the ball only once more that day. The Raiders lost 16-10. "I haven't been this disappointed since I tore my shoulder my junior year at Auburn," Bo said.

Bo was unable to play in the Raiders' final two games. He finished his first season with 554 yards rushing and six touchdowns. Bo's average gain of 6.8 yards rushing per carry was the best in the league, and he was later named the NFL Rookie of the Year.

Bo had proved that he belonged in the NFL, and the Raiders were eager to have him play for them again in 1988. "We've only seen the tip of the Bo Jackson iceberg," said Raider defensive back Mike Haynes. "I've been around some great athletes, but I've never seen anyone like him. I just hope he decides to play for us instead of the Royals."

Many people thought Haynes would get his wish. Bo's

contract with the Royals would end after the 1988 season. There seemed to be no reason why Bo would want to be booed as a Royal when he could be cheered as a Raider. The Royals had also said that Bo would have to prove to them that he was serious about baseball.

"Bo has to decide if he wants to be a baseball player or not," said Avron Fogelman, one of the owners of the Royals, that winter. "We have no interest in continuing this circus. Frankly, I think Bo will have a tough time starting for our team next season."

John Schuerholz added, "The tail wagged the dog last year. It won't happen again. We aren't going to screw up our team if there is any question about Bo. I don't know right now if he'll play the 1988 season at Kansas City. He may play for the [Triple A] Omaha Royals instead."

John Wathan, who was the new manager of the Royals, said, "We know Bo might quit if he is sent to the minors, but we'll have to live with that."

Reporters then asked Bo if he still wanted to play baseball. "I'm not going to make any announcements," Bo said. "I've already made enough announcements in my life. Come to spring training and find out."

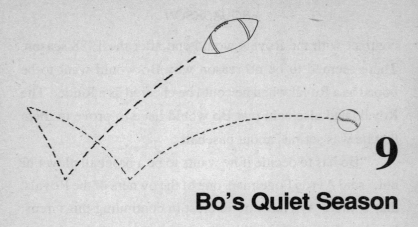

9

Bo's Quiet Season

When Bo arrived at the Royals' spring training camp in Florida in February of 1988, he had a Raiders license plate on his Mercedes-Benz. He was also six days early and he did not want to talk to reporters.

"There was plenty said about me this winter, so I'll just keep quiet and let those same people talk," Bo said. "I'm trying to forget all about last year. All I'm concerned about is 1988."

Bo was concerned because a rookie named Gary Thurman was challenging his job as the Royals' starting leftfielder. Thurman had replaced Bo late in the 1987 season and he had batted .296 in 27 games. He had also spent the winter playing baseball in Puerto Rico to prepare for his battle with Bo that spring.

"Bo is a celebrity and I know he's the one that people want to see," Thurman said. "We're best of buddies, but this is business. All I want is my chance."

Bo was not afraid to be sent to the minors. His agent had told the Royals that Bo was willing to play in the lowest league in baseball. However, Bo was not about to give up his job without a fight.

When the rest of the Royals arrived in camp a few days later, they were surprised to find Bo taking extra batting practice and quietly working hard. "We all know that he doesn't need baseball," said Royals outfielder Thad Bosley. "With his talent and ability in football, he could say, 'See you all later, I'm gone.' But he's here."

George Brett said, "There will be a lot more pressure on Bo this year because he has to make the team. But Bo knows what he has to do and he is willing to accept the challenge. I wouldn't bet against him. When Bo looks in his crystal ball, he doesn't see Omaha. He sees Kansas City."

Bo might have seen Omaha in his crystal ball after he struck out 10 times in his first 23 at-bats that spring. Luckily, he had time to recover because John Wathan had said that he would not decide whether or not Bo had made the team until the end of spring training. Bo then began to hit. Three weeks later, his batting average was .333!

Wathan was encouraged by Bo's performance. "I see steady improvement," he said. "He's fielding his position, catching the ball, and learning the strike zone. Last year, Bo often swung at high pitches that were above the letters on his uniform. Nobody can hit those pitches. Major league pitchers aren't dumb. They'll throw high pitches to a hitter as long as they keep getting him out."

Pitchers did not get Bo out very often that spring. He batted .298 and led the Royals in home runs with five. Bo was then named the team's starting leftfielder. Gary Thurman, who had batted only .185, was told to pack his bags for Omaha.

"Bo had a good spring training camp last year, too, but this year he's even better," said George Brett. "He's worked extemely hard. A lot of times, I would get to the ballpark at 8:15 in the morning and Bo would already be in the batting cage, hitting."

John Schuerholz said, "Bo did everything we asked of

him. He was dedicated to reaching his goal of making this ballclub."

Bo's teammates appreciated his effort and they apologized for the way they had treated him. "I was upset last year and I said some unfortunate things," Willie Wilson said. "When he needed us most, we abandoned him. He deserves another chance. Right now, Bo's a baseball player and he's here to help us win baseball games."

Bo did not hear about football very much that spring except when fans shouted, "How's Al Davis?" or "Tackle him, Bo!" In fact, Bo expected the Royals fans to boo him when he played his first game at Royals Stadium on April 4, 1988.

Opening Day began poorly for Bo. He got stuck in traffic on the way to the ballpark and he arrived after his teammates had begun to warm up. John Wathan then fined Bo $250. "There's no excuse for him not being here on time," Wathan said. "Everyone else got here."

Bo then prepared himself for the boos. When he ran out to leftfield at the start of the game, Bo was surprised when the crowd of 40,648 fans gave him a standing ovation. They even cheered after he struck out during his first time at bat!

Bo heard louder cheers when he smacked a double to rightfield in his second at-bat.

The Royals lost 5-3 to the Toronto Blue Jays that day, but Bo saw an important difference in himself. "I'm more relaxed this year," he said after the game. "The work I've done this spring made me a better ballplayer."

Bo made that clear during the first two months of the season. He got four hits against the Boston Red Sox on April 22. He stole three bases against the Milwaukee Brewers on April 29. In May, Bo got at least one hit in 21 of his 27 games. He also hit five homers, drove in 19 runs, and stole nine bases. He was then named the Royals' Player of the Month.

By the time the Royals went to Cleveland, Ohio, to play the Indians on May 31, Bo was batting .309 with nine home runs and 30 runs batted in. He had also thrown out more base runners (nine) than any other American League outfielder. Unfortunately, Bo's hot start cooled that night.

Bo was running to first base when he tore the hamstring in his left leg. A hamstring is a muscle that runs up and down the back of the thigh. Bo's injury was so painful that he had to walk on crutches. The doctors told him that he would not be able to play for at least six weeks.

"Bo was just about to become a star for good when that happened," said John Wathan. "He had it all together."

Bo's injury was one of the most serious he had ever suffered, but he recovered quickly, just as he had after he separated his shoulder in college. Bo was able to play again in only 32 days and he rejoined the Royals on July 2.

Bo picked up right where he had left off. On July 16, at Fenway Park against the Boston Red Sox, he blasted a towering home run that hit the top of a 70-foot-high wall in centerfield. He later made a spectacular running catch of a line drive to left centerfield. "I didn't think anybody in the world had a prayer of catching it," said Royals pitcher Mark Gubicza [*GOO-ba-zah*].

After that, Bo began to slump. He batted only .203 from the beginning of July through early August, and Peter Gammons of *Sports Illustrated* wrote that Bo was playing poorly because he had "Pigskin on the Brain."

Bo's teammates continued to support him. They did not even mind when he gave them Raider hats and T-shirts. "I have all the confidence in the world in him as a baseball player," said Mark Gubicza. "He's totally committed to the sport he's playing at that particular time."

John Wathan said, "I'm very happy with Bo. I think the football thing is in the past. He's just one of the guys now." Bo was very glad to hear that. "It's what I always wanted," he said.

Bo did not play well again after his injury that season. In his final 78 games, Bo batted only .205 and he tied a Royals record by striking out nine times in a row! Royals hitting coach Mike Lum knew what was wrong. "After the injury, Bo started putting a lot of pressure on himself to play well again," Lum said. "That's where the strikeouts came from."

Bo finished the season with a .246 batting average and 146 strikeouts in 439 at bats. Even though he had struggled during the second half of the season, Bo had shown signs of great promise.

He had thrown out more base runners (11) than any other Royals outfielder. Even though he had missed a month of the season due to injury, he had still hit 25 home runs and had stolen 27 bases. Those totals made Bo the first Royals player ever to hit 25 or more homers and steal 25 or more bases in one season!

"Bo's going to hit 40 home runs and steal 40 bases some year," George Brett predicted. "Then he's going to score 40 touchdowns!"

Scoring touchdowns was Bo's next job, and his mind was on football when he reported to the Raiders on October 12, 1988. "I left the Royals in Kansas City, and I'll see them whenever," Bo told reporters that day. "I'd rather not talk about them."

The Raiders were happy to have Bo back. They had lost four of their first six games and they needed him. "He's so fast, it's unbelievable," said Raider offensive tackle Don Mosebar. "Now other teams can't concentrate on Marcus Allen all the time. We have another great threat."

After his first practice, Bo declared that he was ready to play. "If we had a game tomorrow, I could play," Bo said. "I know the plays. I'm not uncomfortable because I'm not a new person around here anymore."

But Bo *was* uncomfortable before he played in his first game for the Raiders that season. Why? The game was against the Chiefs and it was played in Kansas City! Bo again expected to hear boos and to have baseballs thrown at him.

To Bo's surprise, the crowd of 78,516 fans in Arrowhead Stadium did not treat him badly — even when he rushed for 70 yards, scored a touchdown, and helped the Raiders beat the Chiefs, 27-17! "It turned out to be different than last year," Bo said. "I didn't know what to expect, but the crowd was wonderful. I saw only one baseball!"

The Raiders' new head coach, Mike Shanahan, had not known what to expect either. Coach Shanahan had said that he didn't think Bo would be ready to play. "I was surprised at the shape that Bo was in," he said. "He looked like he got stronger as the game went on."

Bo had a strong start against the New Orleans Saints the next week, and he gained a total of 45 yards during his first two carries. Then he hurt his leg and he had to leave the game. The Raiders lost 20-6.

Bo returned against the Chiefs the next week, and he ran 22 yards for a touchdown the first time the Raiders had the ball. The Raiders won, 17-10, but that touchdown was Bo's last of the season.

Bo played in each of the Raiders' next six games, but he did not get many chances to run with the ball. Coach Shanahan liked to use many different players on offense, so Bo had to share playing time with running backs Marcus

Allen and Steve Smith. Bo carried the ball an average of only 13 times in each of his 10 games that season and gained a total of 580 yards rushing.

One of Bo's best games that season was as a receiver. On December 4, he gained 138 yards by catching six passes to help the Raiders beat the Denver Broncos, 21-20. That victory put the Raiders in a tie for first place in the Western Division of the American Football Conference. However, they lost their last two games and failed to make the playoffs.

Bo's season with the Raiders had been quiet and un-spectacular, just like his season with the Royals had been. His final statistics were not dazzling, but Bo had proved that he was dedicated to both baseball and football, and that he could be accepted by his teammates on both the Royals and the Raiders.

Of course, Bo still had to prove that he could excel in both sports. There were many people who had said that he couldn't do it.

"The time will come very soon when Bo has to decide to become a baseball player or a football player," John Schuerholz said. "He would be a much better baseball player if he wasn't playing two pro sports."

George Brett agreed. "I think Bo is going to have to make a decision. If he ever wants to make the Hall of Fame in baseball, he's going to have to devote a little more time. If he wants to make the Hall of Fame in football, he'll have to play a full season in the NFL."

Pro Football Hall of Fame running back Jim Brown agreed. "Bo has to decide what sport he's going to play. The problem I see is he is playing only half a season of football. I don't see his determination to be great."

Johnny Parker, the respected strength-training coach of the New York Giants, agreed. "As great an athlete as Bo is, I just don't see how he can do it."

Bo, of course, had a different opinion. He disagreed. And in 1989, he proved that he was right.

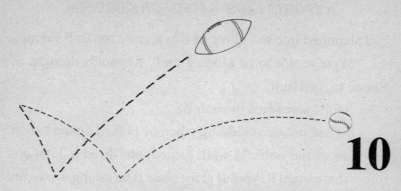

10

Bo Puts It All Together

The Royals and the Seattle Mariners were tied 3-3 in the bottom of the 10th inning on June 5, 1989. There were two outs and Harold Reynolds, who was the Mariners' fastest runner, was on first base. Mariners catcher Scott Bradley then hit a line drive to the wall in the leftfield corner.

As Reynolds rounded second base and headed for third, he could see that Bo was still dashing after the ball. "The game's over," Reynolds said to himself. He then rounded third and sprinted for home plate.

Reynolds was a few feet from home when he noticed that his teammate, Darnell Coles, was frantically signaling that he should slide. "What?" Reynolds said. Suddenly the ball slammed into the glove of Royals catcher Bob Boone.

"You've got to be kidding me!" Reynolds thought as Boone tagged him.

"Out!" screamed the umpire.

Bo had not been kidding when he picked up the ball at the base of the outfield wall, turned, and fired a 300-foot throw that caught Reynolds at the plate. The inning was over, and the Royals later won 5-3.

"It's crazy!" Reynolds said after the game. "I was there. I was the one who was thrown out. I've seen the replay and I still don't believe it. I'm telling you right now, that guy is superhuman."

The word "superhuman" was often used to describe Bo Jackson during the 1989 baseball season. On April 22, Bo went to bat in the seventh inning against Boston Red Sox pitcher Roger Clemens. Clemens had struck Bo out 9 of the 13 times they had faced each other.

"I'm going to get him," Bo said to a teammate before he went to bat. Sure enough, Clemens fired a 93-mile-per-hour fastball and Bo blasted it for a home run.

"He'd never shown that he could hit that pitch," Clemens said. "I had a lot on that ball, but I tip my hat to him. He whistled his bat through the strike zone like nothing I'd ever seen, and he hit the ball so hard I couldn't even turn around to see it go over the fence!"

Pitcher Nolan Ryan of the Texas Rangers felt the same way on May 23 after Bo smashed one of his fastballs 461 feet for the longest home run ever hit at Arlington Stadium. Ryan had struck Bo out six times in a row. That was nothing for Bo to be ashamed of because Ryan had struck out more than 5,000 hitters during his career, more than any major league pitcher in history.

Ryan's first two pitches had been 95-mile-per-hour fastballs that whistled dangerously close to Bo's head. Bo stood in the batter's box, popped his gum a few times, and stared at Ryan. Two pitches later, Bo blasted his home run.

"This is not a normal guy," George Brett said. "He's superhuman. Every day, he does something that opens your eyes."

Bo opened the eyes of players, fans, and sportswriters during the 1989 season. He was at last doing all the spectacular things so many people had expected him to do.

By May 23, Bo was leading the Royals with 12 home runs, and he had 28 runs batted in and 15 stolen bases. If Bo continued to play at this level, he would become the second player in major league history to ever hit 40 homers and steal 40 bases in the same season. Jose Canseco of the Oakland A's in 1988 had been the first.

More important, Bo was striking out less and his defense had improved. "He's made two great catches this season on balls hit over his head, which is the hardest play for a leftfielder to make," John Wathan said. "A year ago, he would never have caught them. His throw against Seattle was the greatest throw I have ever seen in my life."

John Schuerholz said, "I would like to say that I'm very surprised at what Bo has done, but I'm not. When we drafted him, we felt he had the best natural baseball ability and the most awesome potential that anybody had ever seen in the history of our team."

Whenever he played that season, Bo dazzled his teammates and the players on other teams. "Bo and Canseco are the guys that everyone wants to watch," said Scott Bradley of the Mariners. "When they're done, you go into the clubhouse and swap stories about balls they've hit. It doesn't matter if we haven't played the Royals for two months, Bo gets talked about."

Willie Wilson said, "Bo is the only baseball player that you sense can do anything he wants to do."

That was true. People no longer talked about Bo as just a baseball and football player. They also wondered if he would play basketball or maybe even join the Olympic team. There did not seem to be anything Bo couldn't do.

Well, actually, there were a couple of things. "Bo doesn't know anything about golf," says Royals pitcher Bret Saberhagen. There was also hockey.

That spring, Bo made his "Bo Knows Sports" commercial. He was shown hitting home runs, running over tacklers, and dunking basketballs. Another version of the commercial even showed him playing soccer and cricket.

Bo was also shown in a hockey uniform as he checked a player into the boards, but Bo wasn't really wearing skates. He wasn't on ice at the time, either. The Royals were afraid Bo might break his ankle if he tried to skate, so he had to wear socks and the scene was filmed in a gym at the University of Kansas. The cameras showed Bo only from the knees up.

It really didn't matter if Bo could skate, anyway. He was dazzling enough in baseball. When the starting lineups of the All-Star teams were announced that summer, Bo had received more votes from fans than any other American League player. "It's an honor, a real good feeling," Bo said. "I'm just happy to be picked, but it doesn't matter if I'm the first guy picked or the last."

Bo was practically a living legend by the time he went to Anaheim, California, on July 10, 1989, for the All-Star Game. Players from the National League were eager to get their first look at him, and National League President Bill White jokingly introduced Bo at a press conference as "Bo Jackson of the Los Angeles Raiders."

"He looks like he's been cut out of rock," said National League outfielder Tony Gwynn of the San Diego Padres.

Later that day, the All-Stars competed in a home run hitting contest. Bo hit only one and he was kidded about it by American League outfielder Kirby Puckett of the Minnesota Twins. "*One* home run, Bo?" Puckett said. "I can't believe that, one home run."

Bo did hit one ball that amazed the players — a smoking line drive off the leftfield wall. "He's incredible," said National League outfielder Kevin Mitchell of the San Francisco Giants. "It's unbelievable how hard he hits the ball."

. Tony Gwynn added, "The ball was 10 feet off the ground. If the fence had been any softer, it would have torn right through it!"

Before the game, American League manager Tony LaRussa of the Chicago White Sox announced that Bo would bat first, or lead-off, for the American League. "I think he gives us a great chance to get on the scoreboard early," LaRussa said.

LaRussa was right. Bo hit a home run as the first American League player to bat in the game. Bo also stopped the National League from breaking the game open in the top of the first inning.

American League pitcher Dave Stewart of the Oakland A's had struggled, and the National League had scored two runs. There were two outs and the National League had runners on first and third when Pedro Guerrero of the St. Louis Cardinals smacked a line drive to leftfield. At first, it looked as if the ball would drop in for a hit and another run would score, but Bo made a nice running catch to retire the side.

Bo did it all that night: good defensive plays, a home run, a stolen base, two runs batted in. No one could complain after he was named the All-Star Game's Most Valuable Player.

After the game, reporters asked Bo how he felt about being the first player since Willie Mays to hit a home run and steal a base in the same All-Star Game. "I don't think about history, but this may be special when I can sit down and tell the story to my grandkids," Bo said. "I hate being compared to players of the past. When people say that you're the next Willie Mays, you can start to believe that. It can go to your head and really mess you up."

Bo's great All-Star Game made him one of the biggest sports stars in the world. His agent received many offers from companies that wanted to make Bo Jackson toys and other products. Reporters kept asking him how it felt to be a legend.

"I'm no legend," he said. "I just want to be looked at as a baseball player."

Bo went on to bat .256 with 32 home runs, 105 runs batted in, and 26 stolen bases that season. He might have done even more if he had not lost his ability to play from July 26 until August 8 because of a leg injury. Bo's leg bothered him the rest of the season and it kept him from reaching 40 home runs and 40 stolen bases. It was clear, however, that it would only be a matter of time until he did.

"There's no telling how good he can be," John Wathan said.

Bo had once again done something that people had said he could not do. "Everyone who doubted Bo from the East Coast to the West Coast made fools of themselves," Bo said.

Bo also enjoyed his best NFL season that year. After only two practices, Bo gained 45 yards against the Kansas City Chiefs for the Raiders' longest run of the season. Against the Washington Redskins, he gained 144 yards, including a 73-yard run. Against the Cincinnati Bengals, he ran 92 yards for a touchdown. It was the longest gain by a running back in Raider history.

Bo thought nothing of it. "My grandmother could have made that run," he said.

Bo finished the season as the Raiders' leading rusher with 950 yards. Eleven NFL running backs gained more yards than he did, but they had all played a full season. Bo had played in only 10 of the Raiders' 16 games.

Just as he had done during the baseball season, Bo won great praise from both his teammates and his opponents. "I don't think there's any question that Bo is the athlete of our time," said Raider defensive end Howie Long. "I feel fortunate to have the experience of playing with him. The great thing about him is that he just does what he wants to do. It has nothing to do with accolades. That's refreshing."

Bengal head coach Sam Wyche said, "Bo is one of the rare ones to come along. I just hope he'll be appreciated as long as he's here. He's going to be talked about as one of the legends of the game, believe me."

Bo, of course, was not surprised that he had done so much in both baseball and football in 1989. "It doesn't surprise me, but it tickles me to see these people now and watch how they are in awe of all the things I do," he said. "I don't consider it anything spectacular or super because I have been doing it since I was in eighth and ninth grade."

It's safe to say that people will no longer tell Bo what he can and cannot do. However, they are eager to have him tell them what he will do next.

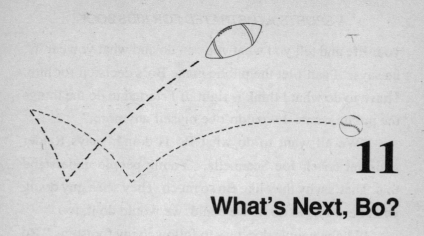

11

What's Next, Bo?

Bo Jackson has certainly come a long way since his days as a neighborhood bully. He has done many spectacular things and he has answered many important questions about himself: Did he want to make something of his life? How good an athlete can he be? How dedicated is he to making the most of his wonderful talents?

Bo has most often answered these questions with actions instead of words. He has succeeded whenever people told him he would fail. Most of all, Bo has refused to change himself or give up his goals, no matter how loudly he has been booed and criticized.

"There are always going to be people who will judge

your life and tell you what you can do and what you can't," he says. "I can't let the public make Bo's decision for him. I have to do what I think is right. If I started to do the things the public wants, I wouldn't be myself anymore."

"We all want to do what Bo is doing," says Raider assistant coach Joe Scannella. "Young people understand this. That's why they like Bo so much. They see a guy doing what he wants to do. If we could, we would do it, too."

"I hope people don't try to follow in my footsteps," Bo says. "My footsteps might be too big for them, or they might be too small for them. A lot of people can act the way I do if they stand up for what is right. I don't think people have the right to say what any human being can accomplish."

No matter what Bo does, or how well he does it, people always want to know what he will do next. They keep asking that question because Bo is such a rare and special athlete. No one has ever been as successful in both baseball and football. As a matter of fact, few athletes have tested themselves the way Bo is testing himself.

Bo must keep his body flexible enough to play 162 games of baseball and strong enough to withstand the pounding of 10 football games. He must also maintain his stamina. Bo can do those things because he does not have to train hard to stay in shape. He is a naturally great athlete.

"Today's athletes train all year long," says Tom Flores, the Raider coach during Bo's first season. "Most never stop working or playing their sport. Many major leaguers play baseball in the winter. You have to be a unique individual to even consider playing two sports at once."

"Bo is unique, there's no question about that," says John Schuerholz. "How long can he do it? Maybe forever. I've never seen an athlete like that."

Even Bo does not know how long he will continue to play two sports. "I know there will be a day when I'll have to choose," he says. "I never meant to be a two-sport athlete for the rest of my life. Baseball is what I will make a career of. Football is the one I will give up. When? I don't know right now. I'll play baseball and football as long as the Good Lord lets me, I guess."

Sometimes even Bo is amazed by the things he is able to do. "I look at myself and wonder, how in the world did I get this way?" he says. "I was born with a lot of blessings."

Perhaps Bo's greatest blessing is his mind. "What separates Bo is how smart he is," says Auburn football

Coach Pat Dye. "You don't step out of baseball for two days and then play football without having a brilliant mind. I never had a player at Auburn who had Bo's ability to learn. If I put something on the blackboard, he would go do it."

"The athletic part of what I do comes easily for me," Bo says. "If I can handle something in my mind, and put my mind to it, I can usually do it."

That is why people like to think about what Bo could do in sports he has not yet tried. "Any morning now we are going to pick up our newspaper and read that Bo Jackson is going to play goalie in the National Hockey League, or point guard in the National Basketball Association, or defense in the Major Indoor Soccer League," sportswriter Mike Downey wrote in *The Sporting News*.

Few people would be surprised if Bo did any of those things. "Bo just has that feeling that he should see how else he can challenge himself," says Tom Flores. "He needs to see if he can conquer another mountain."

Bo wants to keep his next mountain a secret. "I like to keep people guessing," he says. "The idea is to never let the public know my next move."

Bo has said that after he retires from sports, he wants

to help kids by starting his own day care center and summer camp. Bo now has a doctoral degree in child development from Auburn University. His wife Linda is a candidate for a doctoral degree in psychology. "Hopefully we can work together," Bo says. "My wife would be the boss. I think she would hire me."

In the meantime, maybe it's time that people stopped asking Bo questions. As sportswriter Mark Heisler wrote in *The Los Angeles Times*, "Are we likely to see anyone like Bo again? Hadn't we better enjoy this while it lasts?"

After all, it is impossible to know what Bo will do next, but you can be certain that he will do it well and in his own way.

"I want to make my own footprints in the sand," he says. "I don't want to walk in anyone else's."

Bo's Statistics

Professional Football

Year	Rushing			Receiving			
	Yards	Avg.	LR*	Yards	Avg.	LR*	TD
1987	554	6.8	91	138	8.5	23	6
1988	580	4.3	25	79	8.7	27	3
1989	950	5.5	92	69	7.7	20	4

* Longest run from scrimmage.

Major League Baseball

1986

Avg.	G	AB	R	H	HR	RBI	SO
.207	25	82	9	17	2	9	34

1987

Avg.	G	AB	R	H	HR	RBI	SO
.235	116	396	46	93	22	53	158

1988

Avg.	G	AB	R	H	HR	RBI	SO
.246	124	439	63	108	25	68	146

1989

Avg.	G	AB	R	H	HR	RBI	SO
.256	135	515	86	132	32	105	172

1990

Avg.	G	AB	R	H	HR	RBI	SO
.272	111	405	74	110	28	78	128

Bo Info

NAME:	Vincent Edward Jackson
BIRTHDATE:	November 30, 1962
BIRTHPLACE:	Bessemer, Alabama
HOMES:	Bessemer, Alabama and Leawood, Kansas

Bo's Favorite Things

FOOD:	Everything
ATHLETE:	Mike Tyson
MOVIE:	*Rain Man*
ACTRESS:	Cicely Tyson
ACTORS:	Bill Cosby and Eddie Murphy
TELEVISION SHOW:	*The Cosby Show*
SINGER:	Aretha Franklin
SONG:	*When A Man Loves A Woman*
COLOR:	Red
CAR:	Ferrari Testarossa™
BOOK:	*The Old Man and the Sea*
CLOTHING:	Jeans and T-shirts
PLACE TO BE:	Fishing
BIGGEST SPORTS THRILL:	Getting college athletic scholarship
PERSON HE WOULD MOST LIKE TO MEET:	Gen. Chuck Yeager

Football Field

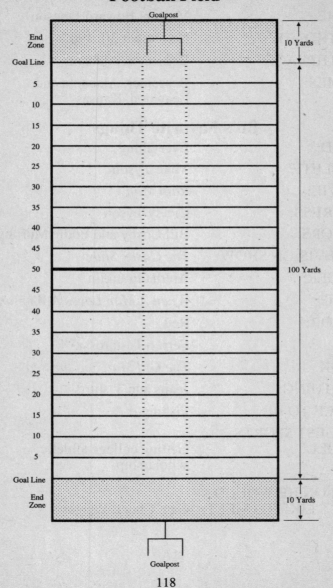

Goalpost

End Zone — 10 Yards

Goal Line

5

10

15

20

25

30

35

40

45

50 — 100 Yards

45

40

35

30

25

20

15

10

5

Goal Line

End Zone — 10 Yards

Goalpost

Football Formations

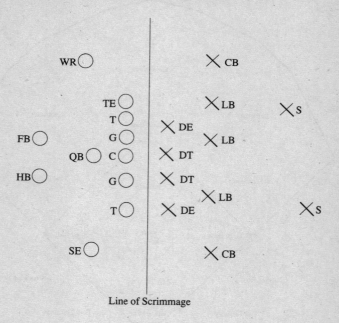

Line of Scrimmage

Offense

FB — Fullback
HB — Halfback
WR — Wide Receiver
QB — Quarterback
TE — Tight End
T — Tackle
G — Guard
C — Center
SE — Split End

Defense

CB — Cornerback
LB — Linebacker
DE — Defensive End
DT — Defensive Tackle
S — Safety

Baseball Field

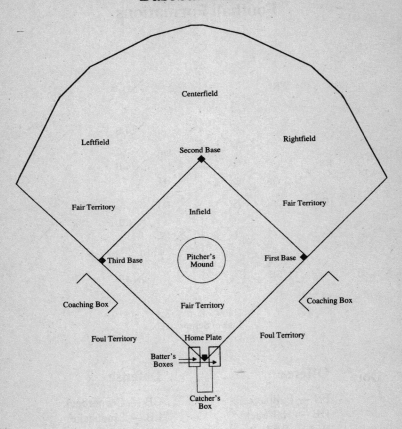

Centerfield

Leftfield

Rightfield

Second Base

Fair Territory

Fair Territory

Infield

Third Base

Pitcher's Mound

First Base

Coaching Box

Coaching Box

Fair Territory

Foul Territory

Foul Territory

Home Plate

Batter's Boxes

Catcher's Box

Glossary
Baseball Terms

All-Star Game: The annual game played between the best players in the National League and the American League. The make-up of each team is based on votes cast by sportswriters, coaches, players, and fans.

Ball: A pitch thrown outside the strike zone.

Base on Balls: Also known as a walk. When the batter advances to first base because four pitches thrown during his at-bat were outside the strike zone.

Bunt: A soft hit that results from the batter holding the bat out and letting the ball hit it, rather than swinging the bat at the ball.

Error: A fielding misplay or wild throw that allows the batter to reach base or a runner to advance.

Hits:
- **Single** – A base hit that allows a batter to reach first base.
- **Double** – A base hit that allows a batter to reach second base.
- **Triple** – A base hit that allows a batter to reach third base.
- **Home Run** – A hit by a player that allows him to round the bases and score a run. Home runs are usually hit over the fence in the outfield.

Minor League: A training league system by which most

players get to the major leagues. Each major league club has its own minor league system (also called farm system). There are four levels in the minor leagues — rookie, A, Double A, and Triple A. The largest number of players are in the rookie league or in the A League. As they get better, they move up through the system toward the major leagues.

Rookie: A player in his first year of a professional sport. To qualify as a rookie in baseball, a player must have at least 130 at-bats, 50 innings, or 45 days of playing in the major leagues before September 1.

Run Batted In: Also called an RBI. A run that scores because of an offensive action by the batter.

Stolen Base: A situation in which a runner on a base is able to run to the next base safely on a pitched ball that the batter takes for either a ball or a strike.

Strike Zone: The area over home plate between the level of the batter's knees and his armpits where the ball must pass to be called a strike, even if the batter doesn't swing.

Football Terms

Block: To stop the movement of an opposing player by hitting him with the shoulders or the body. Offensive blocking prevents the defense from reaching the carrier.

Down: Each offensive play is termed a down. Players on the offensive team have four downs to move the ball at least 10 yards. If they make 10 yards or more before their fourth down, they begin again with another first down. If they don't move the ball 10 yards within four downs, they must turn the ball over to the opposing team.

End Zone: A 10-yard-deep area at both ends of the field between the goal line and the end line. A player must cross the goal line into the end zone with the ball to make a touchdown.

Extra Point: After a touchdown, there is a chance for the scoring team to make an additional point by placekicking, passing, or running the ball into the end zone.

Forward Pass: A forward throw from the quarterback to a receiver.

Fumble: When a ball carrier drops the ball. The ball is still in play after a fumble and either team may recover the ball.

Goal Line: A line that stretches the width of the field, marking the beginning of the end zone. A player must carry or catch the ball behind this line in order to score a touchdown.

Kicking:
 •**Placekick** – A kick in which the ball is held on the ground or placed in a kicking tee and then kicked. Often used for kickoffs, field goals, and extra point attempts.
 •**Punt** – A kick in which the ball is dropped from the hands and is kicked before the ball reaches the ground. This is usually done when the offensive team has a fourth down.

Lateral Pass: When the ball is thrown parallel to the line of scrimmage or away from the offensive goal line.

Line of Scrimmage: An imaginary line parallel to the goal lines that marks the spot to which the ball was carried on the last play. The offense starts the next play from this line.

Rushing: The act of moving forward toward the end zone by running with the ball.

Sack: To tackle the opposing quarterback behind the line of scrimmage before he can pass the ball.

Scoring:

- **Field Goal** – A score of three points made by placekicking the ball through the goalposts and over the crossbar.
- **Point After** – After a touchdown is scored, the team has the opportunity to score an extra point. The team lines up on the 2 1/2 yard line, and the center snaps the ball to the holder, who sets up the ball for the placekicker. The kicker tries to kick the ball between the goalposts and over the crossbar. It is worth one point.
- **Safety** – When a member of the offensive team is tackled with the football in his own end zone, it is worth two points for the defense.
- **Touchdown** – A score of six points that is made by carrying the ball or completing a pass over an opponent's goal line.

Tackle: To throw or knock the ballcarrier to the ground, stopping him from going forward.